IN PRAISE OF
JOE HALDEMAN

"If there was a Fort Knox for science fiction writers who really matter, we'd have to lock Haldeman up there."
Stephen King

"Haldeman is a master builder who can fashion future worlds and plots with equal skill."
Publishers Weekly

"His prose is as clear and engaging as his ideas."
The New York Times

"Haldeman's command of the science involved —including the language with its idioms and humor—is outstanding."
San Jose Mercury

Other Avon Books by
Joe Haldeman

ALL MY SINS REMEMBERED
MINDBRIDGE
WAR YEAR

TOOL OF THE TRADE

JOE HALDEMAN

AVON BOOKS ✦ NEW YORK

AVON BOOKS
A division of
The Hearst Corporation
105 Madison Avenue
New York, New York 10016

Copyright © 1987 by Joe Haldeman
Front cover illustration by Joe DeVito
Published by arrangement with the author.
Library of Congress Catalog Card Number: 86-31216
ISBN: 0-380-70438-2

Published in hardcover by William Morrow and Company, Inc.; for information address Permissions Department, William Morrow and Company, Inc., 105 Madison Avenue, New York, New York 10016.

First Avon Books Printing: June 1988

AVON TRADEMARK REG. U.S. PAT. OFF. AND IN OTHER COUNTRIES, MARCA REGISTRADA, HECHO EN U.S.A.

Printed in the U.S.A.

K-R   10   9   8   7   6   5   4   3   2   1

Traveling in the Soviet Union, I was surprised to find, every now and then, KGB and Intourist representatives who could unbend a little and temper their reflexes of suspicion and defensiveness toward Americans. If I named them, it would not help their careers, but this book is dedicated to them, with gratitude for adding a humane dimension to what was often a rather bleak and scary experience.

Special thanks to the KGB man (or woman) who went to lunch (or was it dinner?) with us in Moscow (Leningrad? Kiev?) and, sitting down smiling, pushed the small flower vase toward me and said in a droll whisper, "Speak clearly."

I hope that humorist finds a bootleg copy of this book. I wouldn't hold out for a Russian translation.

Have you noticed that the most subtle shedders of blood have almost always been the most civilized gentlemen? . . . if civilization has not made man more bloodthirsty, it has at least made him more hideously and abominably bloodthirsty. Formerly he saw bloodshed as an act of justice, and with a clear conscience exterminated whomever he thought he should. And now we consider bloodshed an abomination, yet engage in this abomination more than ever.

—FYODOR DOSTOYEVSKY
Notes from the Underground

PROLOGUE

NICK

THEY WOULD BE watching the airport. Couldn't go back there. Try Amtrak? The bus depots? I stepped out of the grubby phone booth and tried to collect my thoughts.

They had Valerie. The man who picked up the phone told me so, in Russian. That was fast work. A good thing I'd had the cab let me off here, several blocks from home.

They won't hurt her. Not until they can get some mileage out of it.

The air was crisp and smelled clean for Boston, traffic staying home with November's first snowfall waiting heavy in the starless sky. Using my hand to occult a streetlamp, I could just see a few flakes darting in the light breeze.

Driving would be hazardous. They say the first snowfall's a bitch even if it's just a flurry. And me not having driven in snow since Iowa, twenty years ago.

Maybe I should take the T up to South Station and get on the first train to anywhere. No. They might have had time to cover it. They might have had time to figure things out. So they could be frightened enough to kill me on sight. Which might be best for all concerned. Might might might. I would find a car.

I could just flag down the next cab and have him take me a few hundred miles. Too conspicuous, though, a hired cab on the interstate at this hour. The KGB couldn't mobilize the Massachusetts Highway Patrol, but it wasn't just the KGB I was worried about. A nice anonymous car would be best. I remembered there was a large parking lot behind the grocery store here on Central Square, and headed toward it.

There was a bar slouching next to the parking lot, not the kind of place I normally frequent, but the broken flickering EATS sign made my stomach growl. I'd only picked at the excellent meal on the Concorde, jetlagged and nervous, and had been running hard since it landed at Dulles. Nobody would be looking for me here, not yet. I could spare a few minutes for a beer and a snack.

The air in the bar was hot and rich with cooking smells—Greek smells, onion and garlic fried in olive oil. The bar had seen better days, probably when Hoover was president. The only remaining sign of elegance past was the long bar of dark oak, expensive detailing slowly eroding under the bartender's cloth. Otherwise the place was all aged Formica and linoleum, dull under the muted glow of plastic pseudo-Tiffany lamps advertising cheap beer. I sat down on the end stool. The brass footrail had holes worn in it from a half century of scuffing.

The woman behind the bar shuffled over and leaned heavily toward me. "What'll it be, honey?" she asked, instantly endearing herself to me. I ordered some pretzels and a beer and, on impulse, a shot of ouzo. There were several brands behind the bar, Greek neighborhood; I picked the one whose name was hardest to pronounce. I said it with a perfect accent and she nodded, unimpressed.

I watched thirty seconds of Gilligan and his island while she drew the beer and selected the proper package of pretzels. She poured a generous shot of ouzo and slid it over. "You're a pr'fessor, right?"

"It's that obvious?"

"Educated guess." She laughed.

I touched the watch and stared at her. "Tell me why."

"You, uh, you said 'please' and, well, you look like the kind of guy who don't go to places like this. You know, tie and all. Like you're, like you're slumming?" She looked confused and moved to the other end of the bar.

I knocked back the shot of ouzo in one hard stab of licorice fire, and shuddered. One brandy after dinner doesn't train you for this sort of thing.

"Stuff'll grow hair on your throat," the other man at the bar said. Late twenties, unshaven, swarthy, wearing a rumpled army-surplus field jacket and incongruous sunglasses.

"Celebrate the first snow," I said, shrugging off my overcoat.

"Teach at Harvard?"

"MIT," I said.

"Engineer?"

"No, psychology. Mechanics of language acquisition. Through semiotics." That should encourage conversation.

"Sem-me-autics," he said, sounding it out. "What's so dangerous about semiotics?"

"What do you mean?" I said, knowing what he meant.

"How come a psychology professor carries a gun?" He had the sort of "directed whisper" that British men cultivate, though his accent was coastal South Carolina. I could hear him clearly from eight feet away, but I was sure no one else could.

"That's annoying," I said softly. "The tailor charged me a great deal. He claimed that only a real pro could spot it."

"There you go," he said with a small proud smirk. "Come on. What's your real racket?"

"Psychology," I said. "Teaching and writing, some consultant work." I actually did publish a paper or two every year on language acquisition and semiotics, but that was a smoke screen, or protective coloration. The Institute would not approve of my most important work, since they have a policy against conducting secret research in defense matters—even if the country you are defending is the United States. In my case, it was not.

"Sure, psychology. If you say so, Doc." He carefully poured beer right up to the rim of his glass.

I stared at him. "And what line of work would you be in? To know about such matters?" He laughed sardonically. "No, really," I said, and kept staring.

He laughed again, nervously this time. "I—this is crazy."

"Yes," I said, and didn't blink.

"I . . . I do lots of things." Dots of sweat appeared on his forehead and upper lip. "I deal dope. Heroin and coke, mostly. Got three girls down in the Zone. Used to do some wet work there. You know."

"I don't know. Tell me about it."

"I—I messed up some people for the, for the local, you know. The Family. Killed one, piece a cake. Piece a fuckin' cake. Back a the head, one shot, pow. From across the room, one shot."

"That's *good*," I whispered. "Do you have a gun with you now?"

"Sure. In this business—"

"Give it to me."

"Hey. I couldn't."

"Walk over here and slip it to me under the bar, where no one can see." He shook his head hard, then eased off the barstool, sidled over, and passed me a small bright-blue automatic. I never took my eyes off him. It works better that way. "Now. Do you have any heroin?"

"Yeah, five bags primo."

"Do you have the means for injecting it?"

"The works, yeah."

"Good. I want you to go into the men's room and inject all of it into yourself."

"Hey. I couldn't take that much even when I was on it. Kill a fuckin' horse."

"Nevertheless, you will do it. Inject it into a vein. In the men's room. Now."

He shook his head but his eyes returned to mine. Then he went back to where his beer was and looked at it, but didn't get back on the stool. *"Now!"* I whispered sharply. He shuffled back toward the men's room.

An unusual degree of resistance. Probably an approach-retreat confusion due to being an ex-addict. Like I feel about cigarettes.

I gave him a few minutes, finishing my beer. A man stood up and headed for the john; I quickly followed him. I got there just in time to block the entrance as he came backing out. He touched me and spun around, agitated. "Hey—there's a guy—"

I put a finger to my lips. "Shh, I know. There's a man throwing up in the toilet. That's what you saw. Disgusting, isn't it?"

He nodded slowly. "Yeah. Guys oughta learn how much they can handle."

"You are going to leave and never come back to this place."

"Yeah. Right."

"Don't forget your coat. Don't forget to pay." You have to cover details like that.

"Sure." I watched him retrieve his coat and reach for his wallet and then turned my attention to the men's room. It was an ugly place, thick purple paint rolled over walls and partitions, the porcelain appliances yellowed and cracked. Smell of old piss and too little cheap disinfectant. I used the urinal from a safe distance.

He was slumped on the toilet with his head between his knees, knuckles on the grimy floor. The hypodermic was still stuck in his forearm, its reservoir full of blood, and a thin trickle of blood ran down to pool in his palm. I put a finger to his carotid artery. The pulse was shallow and irregular.

It stopped. I shoved the body back into a more upright posture, so it wouldn't be discovered right away. Like hauling on a bag of grain, hard work for a man my age. There was some blood on the floor but I scuffed it into amalgamation with the background dirt. A wad of paper served to jam the stall door closed.

I went back to the bar and signaled the bartender. She came over, and I leaned close. "What do I look like?" I asked softly.

"What?"

I stared at her. "Describe me, please."

"Tall guy. White, bushy white beard, well dressed—"

"No. I am black, short, bald, and wearing work clothes. Greasy jeans and an Exxon shirt that says Freddy on the pocket. Right?"

"Exxon shirt with Freddy on the pocket."

"Good." I looked down the row of booths and found a likely prospect, a young man with a parking-lot ticket sticking out of his shirt pocket. He was sitting next to a pretty girl who was drinking diet soda from a can; he had a draft beer. They were talking quietly.

I sat down across from them. "Hey," he said. "What—"

I turned it up. "How much have you had to drink?"

"Just this one beer."

"Good. Come on, we're going for a drive."

He scratched his head. "Okay. Where to?" Good question. They'd expect me to go to New York; especially the KGB. They seem to think all the rest of the country is a suburb of Manhattan.

"North. Up to Maine."

"What part?"

"I don't know. I've never been there."

"What about me?" the girl said. "Can I come along?"

I hesitated. It might be slightly safer for me that way, if not for her. Willing hostage. "If we left you here, could you get home all right?"

"Sure. My father's the cook."

"You go home with your father. Tell him—what's your name?"

"Richard."

"Tell him Richard had to leave early, to pick up some medicine for a sick friend. He'll be out of town for a few days. And you never saw me. Never at all."

She looked vaguely through me, focusing on the TV set at the end of the bar. "Uh-huh. Bye, Rich."

I left a couple of dollars on the table. Then we put on our coats and walked out into the swirling night.

CHAPTER ONE

THE MAN WHO calls himself Nicholas Foley—Dr. Nicholas Foley, a full professor in MIT's psychology department—was born Nikola Ulinov, in Leningrad, in 1935. It was not the best time to grow up there.

Leningrad is the most European of Soviet cities, partly from cultural tradition and partly from simple propinquity to Europe. Finland is not too long a drive away, and today, people who are allowed to can cross over into Helsinki and buy computers and jazz records and play roulette for Finnish charities. Finns seem to like Russians now, or at least tolerate them.

But they were not fond of the Russians after Stalin's 1939 invasion, and so it was Finnish soldiers who reinforced Hitler's battalions, converging on Leningrad on the eve of Nikola Ulinov's sixth birthday. Leningrad was ready for them. There weren't many Soviet soldiers there—Stalin, having no love for the European city, had drawn most of the troops toward Moscow for the coming winter—but the civilians had been trained in street-fighting techniques. Molotov cocktails were mass-produced and distributed. Weapons oiled and ammunition portioned out. The people were ready to defend their city street by street against the implacable enemy. If the Nazis wanted Leningrad badly enough, they would no doubt have it. But they would first pay a terrible price.

Hitler, or his advisers, outmaneuvered the Soviets. They saw there was no need to go into the city and fight. All you had to do was cut off all avenues of supply, and let the natives try to live through a Russian winter without food or fuel. Throw in some artillery. At least a third of the city's three million would die. And then when spring came, simply lift the siege, and push the survivors out to disrupt the rest of the Soviet Union.

The strategy did take Leningrad by surprise, but it didn't work out quite as neatly as Hitler had hoped. More than a million did die, but the others didn't cave in. They lived on moldy grain and shoe leather and hope and hate—until three Russian winters finally did to Hitler what one had done to Napoleon. Leningrad and Russia won, even if the price they paid would warp the city and the country with grief and fear for the rest of the century.

(Leningrad's reward for heroism was to become a noncity populated by nonpersons. Malenkov and Beria implemented Stalin's distaste for the Western city by destroying, or hiding in inaccessible archives, all written records of the Siege.)

Five-year-old Nikola knew there was a war going on, and like most boy children, he vaguely approved of the idea. Even when the artillery and bombs began dropping into the city, when sleep was pinched off by air-raid sirens—even then, it provoked excitement more than fear. An interesting game with obscure rules.

Then one day at noon an artillery round or a bomb fell across the street, and Nikola ran outside breath-

less with excitement, and saw his best friend's father
stumbling bloodsoaked out of the wreckage of their
flat, carrying cradled in his arms what was left of his
son, blown to bloody rags and dying there in front of
Nikola with a last bubbling moan. From then on he
would remember the war as quite real, and terrible.
And some parts would be too terrible to remember.

The Leningraders tried to get their children out of
the city before the fighting started in earnest. Nikola
loaded a suitcase almost as big as he was aboard a
boxcar headed for the relative safety of Novgorod.
They never made it. Nazi Messerschmitts, perhaps
thinking it was a freight train, bombed and strafed the
children unmercifully. Nikola's suitcase may have
saved him; at any rate, the clothes and foodstuffs inside absorbed two bullets while he cowered behind it
in the screaming dark. (Forty years later Nick Foley
would still have trouble facing a locker room, or any
such crowded sweaty place. The source of the small
anxiety attacks was a mystery to him, which he accepted along with other small mysteries.)

The Messerschmitts finally ran out of ammunition.
A nearby farming community took care of Nikola and
the other surviving children for a couple of weeks,
and then a night convoy of blacked-out trucks and
ambulances took them back to Leningrad. The children were to be rerouted east to Kirov and Sverd-
lovsk, and most of them did make it. Nikola didn't.
He found himself suddenly without a family, and
while that problem was being straightened out, the
last train left.

His mother and father might have been alive at that
time, but Nikola would never know. They had been
arrested by the NKVD, imprisoned as spies for Nazi
Germany.

It was not impossible. His father was a German

citizen who had immigrated to Russia in the twenties, declaring great sympathy for the Revolution and even changing his name from Feldstein to Ulinov. He had been a philology professor at Heidelberg; in due course he joined the philology department at Leningrad State University.

So to a certain cast of mind, he was triply not to be trusted: an intellectual, a German, a Jew. Why would a German Jew, however lapsed in his religion, want to spy for Hitler? This was not the kind of question that much bothered that cast of mind. Ulinov and his wife were locked up pending transfer to Lubyanka, the forbidding prison in Moscow, but they never made the trip. Sometime during the siege, they either starved to death or were executed. The records claimed execution but, perversely, that status was sometimes conferred after the fact. An informal quota system.

It would be many years before Nikola would know any of this. The authorities explained that his parents had been taken from him by the Nazis, and he had no reason to question that.

Having missed the exodus, Nikola wound up living with Arkady Vavilov, who had been his father's elderly boss, and the old man's wife. He could hardly have found better surrogate parents than the Vavilovs. Missing their own grown children, they showered love and attention on him. What was more important to Nikola's tortuous future, though, was the fact that Vavilov was a linguist and a language teacher. And both the Vavilovs spoke English—American English, having spent years in New York.

Foreign languages were nothing new to the boy. Nikola's parents had brought him up to be equally fluent in German and Russian, and found that he was a thirsty sponge for languages. Professor Ulinov had amused himself by teaching the boy basic vocabularies in French, Japanese, and Finnish. His surrogate father added a little to two of those, but concentrated on the language of those strange folks who would eventually bring the Soviet Union the Lend-Lease Act and other problems.

Vavilov had lots of time, since his part of the university had been shut down. They made a game, if a rather grim one, out of the English lessons. When Arkady or his wife finally came home from the long ration line, they would take Nikola's portion of the bread (and much of their own, which he would never know) and carefully divide it into sixteen equal portions. Each piece would be a reward for a lesson properly recited. Hunger turned out to be an effective aid to what would later be called "the acquisition of languages"—especially during the hardest times, when an individual's bread ration was down to four ounces a day. When the siege lifted after nine hundred days, Nikola was not quite nine years old, but his English was better than that of most Americans a couple of years older. This did not escape the government's attention for long.

During the course of the war, for reasons that were important at the time, the NKVD that had presided over Nikola's parents' deaths changed its initials to NKGB. In March of 1946, it became the MGB, and it was the MGB who came looking for young citizens fluent in English. In 1949 it latched on to fourteen-year-old Nikola Ulinov, with his huge vocabulary, impeccable grammar, and pronounced Bronx accent.

They would have to work on the accent, but otherwise he was perfect. A leader in the local Komsomol, he was an almost fanatic patriot. (In the jargon of his ultimate profession, you might say that he was *fixated* on Soviet Communism as an *outlet* for the *militant enthusiasm* that was the *external manifestation* of the tensions generated by his *frustrated adolescent sexuality* and *ambiguous self-image*.) Other factors: He didn't look at all Russian, with his mother's Aryan features and blond hair. He had no living relatives. He had been toughened by war and privation; like all Leningraders he had seen a thousand faces of death, and you either learned to live with that terrible knowledge or went mad. Nikola seemed to be bleakly sane.

He would make a magnificent spy.

The MGB had gone to a great deal of trouble and expense to build an ersatz American small town in the middle of an Azerbaijan wheat field. It was called Rivertown and was supposed to be in Kansas.

The people who went there were only allowed to speak Russian once a week (a "self-criticism" session, but most of them looked forward to it). A few older ones ran shops or taught school or acted as policemen, firemen, and so forth. Seven of the schoolteachers were transplanted Americans who had grown up in the Midwest. They taught English and history, but mainly they taught:

> How to sit in a public place
> When to defer to adults, and when to be rebellious
> How to use a knife and fork
> The various kissings and touchings appropriate for different stages of a relationship
> How to behave in a public bathroom or shower
> How to spend money
> What things a small-town boy or girl from Kansas would not know

It was a stressful life, but had its advantages. Meat at least twice a day, when most Russians were lucky to see it once a week. American cars for learning how to drive. A library full of books, most of which were not available to the rest of the country's schoolchildren. Coke and coffee, imported at some expense.

Nikola, who was now called Nicky or Nicholas, grew to dread seeing those seven hawk-eyed American mentors. When they weren't around, he could play his part perfectly, but as soon as one of them looked at him, his accent would slip or he would stand too close to someone, talking; hold his coffee cup wrong; forget to cross his legs; cuss or not cuss in the wrong situation. All seven of these foreigners reported directly to the MGB, and Nicky had no illusions as to what the MGB could do to people who disappointed them. He didn't know the seven considered him their star pupil.

He had useful talents aside from playacting and academics. One that could have cut his espionage career short was marksmanship: he had uncanny ability with a pistol. He was almost drafted for the 1952 Olympics, but the MGB held on to him. Linguist, pistol shot, ballroom dancer—if he could only tell one wine from another, he could have been a regular James Bond.

They couldn't make a mathematician out of him, though, which frustrated the MGB's plans. They had wanted to insert him into the United States after he'd finished Rivertown High, to excel in physics or engineering and eventually wind up in a sensitive research position. But calculus was a smooth unclimbable wall to him. Reluctantly they decided to let him follow his natural leanings.

So as his eighteenth birthday approached, they assembled a dossier that gave Nicholas Foley a complete and tragic past. Found abandoned soon after birth, Nicky was raised in an orphanage in Lawrence, Kansas. The orphanage is one that actually did exist, but it burned to the ground, along with all records, in 1947. Nicky survived and was adopted by Neil and Pamela Foley, who died together in an automobile accident in 1952. (None of this tragedy was arranged by Soviet intelligence, who don't make a practice of murdering innocent foreigners; they just studied a few Kansas newspapers.) The court appointed a guardian for Nicky, but he ran away.

A few days before his eighteenth birthday, Nick got off an Aeroflot plane in Toronto, bluffed past customs, then wandered around the city for a couple of days making sure he wasn't being followed. He took a bus to Ottawa and a train back. He crossed the border at Niagara in a Greyhound, got on the train in Buffalo, and in three days wound up in Lawrence, Kansas, where he walked to the Selective Service office and volunteered for the draft.

Two years in the post-Korea American army did nothing to shake his faith in the Soviet system (a stint in the Soviet army might have); he was possibly the best Communist ever to earn the Good Conduct Medal and go to school on the GI Bill. And go to school he did, as prearranged: B.A., Psychology, University of Kansas, 1959; M.A. Linguistics, University of Iowa, 1961; Ph.D. Psychology, also Iowa, 1963. He settled in to teach in Iowa City and wait for his first assignment. It would be two years in coming.

CHAPTER TWO

NICK

I ARRIVED IN Cambridge more than twenty years ago, glad to be escaping the Iowa winters, looking forward to the intellectual stimulation and challenge I knew the MIT and Harvard communities would provide—and also looking forward to my first meeting with an actual American Office KGB agent. Though technically I was one myself, of course.

I'd studied and taught at Iowa for almost six years without so much as a cryptic postcard. Then one night I was working late at the office grading finals, and a woman walked in, smiled, handed me an envelope, and left without a word. In the envelope was a clipping from the *Journal of Educational Psychology* advertising an opening for an assistant professor at MIT. I applied and got the job right away.

(That's one problem with this kind of life. When things go well, you can never be sure whether it's good luck and reward for ability, or strings being pulled on your behalf. Another problem, obviously, is paranoia, and I would soon have advice about that.)

A small stack of mail was waiting for me at MIT, mostly journals and advertising circulars. There was also a note in an envelope with no return address:

"We must talk. Let us have a picnic at Walden Pond on Thursday, September 9th. Meet me at noon by the ruins of the cabin. Bring a bottle of red wine.—VL"

Over the past twenty years, most of my contacts with Vladimir Lubenov—or anybody else from the KGB—have been outdoors, even when it meant standing in ten-degree weather with the snow falling horizontally. This first meeting, though, was pleasant: a place of quiet beauty, leaves changing color, surprisingly few people. There was only one person at the rectangle of stones that marked the place where Thoreau had lived so economically, and he was holding a picnic basket. We shook hands American style and he introduced himself. I started to say something in Russian, but he cut me off with a sharp jerk of his head and then a self-effacing laugh. "Paranoia, Nicholas. Paranoia is its own reward." He had a rather thick Russian accent, Moscow.

We took basket and bottle up to the top of a small rise, where we could see for quite a distance in every direction—something we certainly wouldn't do today. They could shine a laser on a nearby leaf and pick up our conversation from its vibrations. Or something.

Over a weird lunch of Chinese-restaurant takeout food and French table wine, Vladimir gave me a broad outline of what I was to do and be for the next few years.

"Of course you are aware," he said, not looking at me, setting out white boxes on a small checkered cloth, "you are aware that our . . . Committee is very changed from the time when you and I went through our training." We were about the same age. "Less use of force. Very little use of force."

"I know. But I didn't miss the Stashinski trial. Nor Khokhlov."

"*Khokh*lov!" He said it like a curse. Khokhlov had been a senior KGB officer who, a few years before, was given an assassination job in West Berlin and, instead of carrying it out, turned himself over to the American authorities. He brought some interesting weapons with him, things you can't buy in a sporting-goods store, not even today. Vladimir looked at me carefully. "Perhaps I can understand his being reluctant to murder a stranger in cold blood. But he could have refused the assignment. This is not 1948."

"Do you think it did much harm?"

"To the KGB, you mean, or the Soviet Union?" I shrugged. "Perhaps it's not a bad thing for our enemies to think us capable of . . . excess. I suppose in that ruthless sense it serves both the Committee and the Motherland. The other side of the coin, though, is that the CIA is of course capable of excess itself. Things like this make it easier for them to justify their actions."

"Did we actually try to kill him afterward? Thallium poisoning?"

"I don't know." He grimaced. "The Thirteenth Department doesn't confide in me. Thallium does seem unnecessarily exotic.

"At any rate, your own assignment is straightforward enough and, for the time being, includes nothing illegal. No thallium assassinations. We want you to function as a 'spotter.' Simply keep your eyes open, looking for people who might be of use to the KGB, inside your part of the MIT academic community."

"People who express Communist sympathies?"

"Yes, of course. Also first-generation Americans from the Soviet Union or Eastern Europe. People in financial trouble, especially. It's easier to buy an American than to convince him ideologically."

"All right. But we didn't go to all this trouble just to put a spotter in MIT's psychology department."

"No. But almost all of MIT is of potential importance. We can't know yet what your ultimate assignment will be. Simply advance in your field and don't do anything politically suspicious. There will come a time, maybe five years, maybe ten, when we will need a man with your credentials, and a spotless record.

"Meanwhile, I will stay in contact with you. Of course it's best that you know as little about me as possible, not even my real name."

"What if I need to get in touch with you?"

"You won't need to, not at this stage of your assignment. At any rate, I don't live in Boston, nowhere near."

"But what if my true identity is discovered?"

"You may go to jail," he said softly, "or be deported. Nothing worse. I wouldn't worry about violence from the CIA or any of the other intelligence agencies, not unless our silent war becomes much noisier.

"Besides, the only law you've broken is that of illegal immigration, which you did ten years ago as a juvenile. And some small lies that might be considered misdemeanors, in connection with maintaining your identity. 'Spotting' isn't high-level espionage; they don't devote that much energy to countering it."

"I suppose. So how will I get the information to you? Meetings like this?"

"Generally not. There are more secure ways. You'll be instructed." He got up suddenly and dusted off his trousers. "It was good meeting you." We shook hands. He turned abruptly, took a couple of steps and turned back. "Oh. Do you still have the pistols from Iowa?" I had coached the ROTC pistol team.

"Yes . . . I don't know whether to—"

"No, don't register them. Better to take the small chance of exposure. We can't afford to have any of our people on that particular list."

"I should keep them, then?"

"In a safe place. One never knows." He checked his watch and then hurried down the leaf-strewn path. I wouldn't see him again for several years.

I sat on the hill for a while thinking and, not having shed my starving-student ways, finished all the chow mein and sweet-and-sour pork, and washed it down with red wine. I still have the basket. It gives me heartburn to look at it.

My instruction as a spotter began the next morning. There was a large MIT Interoffice Memo envelope on my desk; inside it was a pad of pale-blue notepaper, matching envelopes, and a long note, handwritten in Russian.

The notepaper was "safe," the note said, purchased in a New York dime store and devoid of fingerprints. Most of my spotting reports would be written on it and then dead-dropped—left in a public place for another agent to pick up, unless a curious child or streetcleaner got there first.

I was to write each report with a different safe typewriter, a cheap one bought in a pawnshop and then disposed of. The respondent suggested that I wipe it clean of fingerprints and leave it inconspicuously in a public place, letting an American thief be my accomplice.

At the time, I was extremely annoyed by the cloak-and-dagger caution of the arrangements. It probably wouldn't be smart to write the reports on MIT letterheads and sign my name to them, but this seemed to be laughably excessive. Now, I'm not so sure. Both sides in this game can be thorough.

So every few months for the next couple of years, I would write a list of a few people who might be useful, along with a paragraph or so of explanation for each. I would seal it in an envelope addressed to a nonexistent place and affix a stamp (many people who would open a plain envelope out of curiosity will virtuously drop a stamped one in the mailbox unopened), and then set it down at the place and time instructed. Usually the drop was in a quiet corner of a fairly busy public place—the back booth of a greasy spoon or an uninteresting exhibit in a museum. I never waited to watch the pickup, though of course I was always on the lookout for Lubinov.

In American-spy parlance I was a "sleeper"—someone who leads a fairly normal life until the KGB orders him activated—as well as a spotter. Technically, I suppose I was also an *agent vlyiyania,* or agent of influence; someone who attempts through friendly discussion to alter the opinions of those around him, to bring them more in line with Soviet principles. This being Cambridge in the sixties and seventies, though, even a doctrinaire Marxist would have looked relatively inconspicuous. And I always tried to be careful to temper my outlook with American conventional wisdom. I could deplore "my" country's presence in Vietnam, for instance, yet proclaim my sympathy for the unfortunate lads who had been drafted to fight there.

But by 1971 I had spent half my life—all of my adult life—in America, and a lot of my pro-American sympathies were not feigned. This is not to say I was no longer a good Communist. That the Revolution survived the enormity of Stalin's crimes proved to me its durability, and its durability implied universality.

But American democracy was also surviving Vietnam, Nixon, and the cultural schism of the sixties, and it seemed to me the system might emerge from these adversities tempered rather than weakened. Perhaps tempered in both senses of the word, amenable to detente and the evolution of a more humane economic system.

(I was convinced that it would have to be evolution here, rather than revolution. If there was going to be another American Revolution, it would be to the right. That's where most of the guns were. Not even the Russian Revolution was fought with ideas alone.)

So by this trick of the mind I was working in the best interests of both my homeland and my adopted country. I suppose that's not a rare accommodation for people in my shoes.

In fact, though, matters of espionage and conflicting allegiances took up little of my time, while I was busy "creating background"—which is to say, pursuing the professional and personal interests of a normal American man. In 1971 I married Valerie, who had been one of my most talented students (she teaches Abnormal at Boston U. now), and although or because we have never had children, our marriage is a model of love and sharing. Of course I never shared with her the basic exotic details of my past and present. Perhaps I should have.

It was a mutual interest in hypnosis that brought Valerie and me together. We happened to sit next to each other at a lecture on the anesthetic uses of hypnotism and found out we were in the same department. We meshed.

MIT reserves the winter break, New Year's Day to early February, for IAP, Independent Activities Period. (Everything that changes my life has three initials.) We decided to work with biofeedback, then fashionable, to see whether a willing subject could put himself into a deeper hypnagogic state by monitoring his own physiological parameters.

As it turns out, I am not a good subject for hypnosis, not being particularly artistic or imaginative or reflective. Valerie was all three—a moody fantasizing artist/musician—and after a week of practice, mutual conditioning, I could put her into a deep trance with a word and a touch. I myself could barely manage a light trance after ten minutes of monotonic reassurance, which was not reflection on her ability as a hypnotist. I couldn't get as deep as she did even when I used illegally acquired barbiturates.

Unsurprisingly, we also experimented a bit with the effect of grass, hash, and LSD on hypnosis—perhaps I was a little old for that sort of thing, but she wasn't, and it *was* the sixties—and there was no consistent result, though we did collect some amusing experiences. (Like the day I delivered a lecture to a hall full of thoughtful blue lizards.)

Valerie had started out majoring in electrical engineering, and although she switched to psych, she never did lose her love for gadgets. I like machines, too, but don't have her talent or creativity. It was her initial fiddling that eventually led to the device that ultimately so complicated our lives.

She had gotten hold of a picoammeter, a machine that measures electrical currents down to a fraction of a trillionth of an ampere. On a dry day you can make the needle move from across the room by running a comb through your hair.

We had both progressed far enough in biofeedback that it was easy for us to isolate our alpha and theta waves by a special kind of "relaxed concentration" that was obviously related to the hypnagogic state. We normally did this with the help of a commercial "brainwave monitor" that used a headband with two electrodes, and an earphone connected to a black box that was some kind of a signal generator working with a couple of bandpass filters that isolated the alpha and theta waves. You would sit quietly in a dark room with the earphone on while the signal generator gave off a soft, high-pitched whine. Once you relaxed the right way—a "way" that can't really be described in words—the signal would start to warble, which meant you were in the alpha or theta state. At first it took ten or twenty minutes to find the right way to feel; eventually it was a matter of seconds.

There was no way to fiddle with the sealed machine (it belonged to the Institute, anyhow) so Valerie set about cobbling together one of our own. That way she could experiment to her heart's content.

That's where the picoammeter came in. One of the odd things you can do with biofeedback is to alter at will the electrical conductivity of your skin. We had it set up so that the picoammeter measured a microscopic current across the back of your hand. You made a mental effort (or not-effort; it required relaxation) to slow the current down, to increase the resistance, and the picoammeter would reward you, through a signal generator, with a musical tone that rose in pitch as the resistance increased. We both tried it in a normal relaxed state first, and then while hypnotized.

I should add that this was long after IAP was over; I'd known Valerie for more than a year. We saw each other socially as well as in the context of this unofficial research—"socially" in a sixties sense, including offhand sexual intimacy. I can imagine what would happen to one of my assistant professors today in that situation, more or less openly sleeping with a student still enrolled in his department.

That is relevant to what happened. The first run-through, I was subject and Valerie was the hypnotist. The results were not impressive; under hypnosis the note rose perhaps a half tone higher than it did in a normal state, the meter showing it wavering around 450 hertz (from a base tone of A/440). When we switched, the results were astounding.

Unhypnotized, Valerie could push the tone up to around 500. But when I put my hand on her cheek and said "Sleep now"—our combination—the tone started to rise very rapidly, covering several octaves in seconds, and winding up as inaudible ultrasound. The meter showed a steady 28,430 hertz.

If I were more of a scientist, I suppose I might have called off the experiment right there, and then taken the equipment apart to find the glitch. What the steady reading implied was that Valerie was able to control the conductivity of her skin to an impossible degree of fineness—or that the signal generator was busted, much more likely. After it hadn't changed for about a half minute, I told Valerie what was happening.

"Interesting," she mumbled. It wasn't the voice she normally had under hypnosis, which was quite clear and alert. I asked her whether she could make it go higher, and she said she was trying.

It didn't add up. The reason we'd rigged the pico-ammeter with an audible output was to make it easier to use the biofeedback "talent," which works best with the eyes closed, as does hypnosis. But human beings aren't able to hear sounds pitched above about 15,000 to 20,000 hertz. (I didn't remember the exact numbers at the time, though I did know that I was myself deaf to any sound above 4,000 hertz, because of ear damage in childhood, the first winter of the Nazi siege.)

That she was exactly controlling a sound she couldn't possibly hear was enough of a mystery. The mystery was doubled by an astounding change in her trance behavior.

Everybody knows that people under hypnosis can't be compelled to do things that are morally repugnant to them, or liable to cause harm. They will either ignore the command or come out of the trance. Valerie and I were occasionally playful with this, or experimental, using an absurd command to create a sort of "half-in/half-out" semitrance. While your brain wrestled with the unexecutable command, you were neither quite hypnotized nor quite normal, a curious feeling.

After a minute of not being able to get a reasonable response from her, I said, "Why don't you strip off all your clothes and go running down Memorial Drive"—and she raised her eyes up at me, apparently out of trance.

"What did you say?" she asked me slowly. I repeated the command, smiling, but she didn't seem amused. She shook her head, brow knit, then stood and stepped out of her sandals, unsnapped her halter and let it fall, and proceeded to roll down her tight jeans and underwear. I thought she was joking, though it was uncharacteristically bold behavior, since the corridor was well populated and the door to the lab had a small window at eye level.

When she'd unrolled the jeans as far as her knees, I laughed and said, "Okay, stop it."

She gasped and stood bolt upright, and then crouched in a reflex posture of modesty, her right hand covering her pubic triangle while her left tried to pull up the jeans, without much success. Finally she duckwalked to behind a lab table, where she couldn't be seen from the outside, and finished the job, blushing and angry. She asked me what the hell was going on.

I described what had happened without attempting to interpret it. She gave me a lighhearted scolding and then puzzled it out: She did have a streak of sexual exhibitionism that she normally kept in check; my suggestion that she flaunt her charms to a few thousand strangers gave her permission to do what her subconscious had desired since puberty. Plus wanting to hurt her prudish father and other such traditional stuff.

I'm no Freudian now and I wasn't one then. To be fair, Valerie might have come up with an explanation closer to the truth if I had not withheld one bit of information—that her behavior had returned to normal as soon as I'd said "Stop it." Secrecy is of course a reflex with me, and this looked like something that was worth hiding.

Our researches wandered into other, not especially productive, directions, and eventually fizzled out when her course of study and legitimate research, in pursuit of her doctorate, became too demanding. But I held on to the signal generator and pursued my own little project. I kept no written records. I never advertised for subjects, but instead used as guinea pigs the students who'd been hired as subjects for my research about resistance to language acquisition. Sometime in the course of each session I would turn on the sound generator, and ask them to do something absurd. If they were puzzled by the request, I would laugh and correct myself.

It turns out that 28,430 hertz is some sort of "characteristic frequency" for most of the population. I could legitimately ask all of my subjects to take a hearing exam, and indeed most of the people for whom the ultrasonic whine was ineffective turned out to have hearing loss in the high frequencies, as I did. The two who seemed to have normal hearing may have been "deaf" ultrasonically; there was no way to test for that.

What happened was not hypnosis. I'm not sure it's even related, except that Valerie had to be in a hypnagogic state to trigger the runaway biofeedback phenomenon that isolated the frequency. You can't hypnotize someone and tell him to jump off a cliff. I can turn on my machine and ask you to jump off a cliff *smiling*, and you'll do it.

CHAPTER THREE

JACOB

THE CIA HAD been keeping an eye on Professor Nicholas Foley since the fall of '78, when a low-echelon American Officer KGB agent came over to our side with an interesting list—thirty men and women who had graduated from "Rivertown," an ersatz American village/training camp in the middle of Azerbaijan. A few of them we'd long since arrested and deported (they'd come to America in the fifties), but a baker's dozen were still here, apparently living out normal American lives. All of them at least middle-aged.

Foley was an interesting case in that he was a fairly prominent person, well respected in his field, which was the intersection of linguistics, psychology, and education. That's not as narrow as it might seem at first: Foreign language is the classic huge failure of modern American education, and anybody who's working on ways to make language learning easier or faster or more palatable to students does get attention. Foley was working on it at a very basic level, trying to psych out patterns of resistance to language learning among older children and young adults.

And in his spare time he was a Soviet spy.

We tailed him and bugged him for a couple of years without getting anything. In fact, we were about to double back—find out how an innocent man's name had gotten on the list—when he accidentally played right into our hands. He did a dead drop of a list of people who might be "turned," and the pickup was one of our own double agents. (The only one, actually, attached to this small office.) There was nothing on the list to identify _him_, of course, but she'd staked out the pickup site with a hidden video camera.

She made a Xerox copy of the list and passed it on to her KGB higher-up. In some best-of-all-possible worlds, we would have assigned tails to everybody on that list. But there are too few agents and too many lists.

Lists. My life is hemmed in by lists and charts, piles of dusty journals and stacks of computer disks. I'm John Jacob Bailey, a senior analyst for the CIA, head of a very small section that covers Boston and its environs. Cambridge is pretty much home to me, since I got my first Russian degree at Harvard. I should have kept at it to the doctorate; now I'd be living a fairly exciting life as an academic. Instead I quit after the master's (Soviet Affairs, Georgetown, '68) and went straight into the State Department and the CIA. Where I _didn't_ go was Vietnam, which claimed many of my contemporaries.

It wasn't just draft-dodging. I guess I was caught up in the Allen Dulles/Kennedy–era romantic notions about espionage. Envisioned myself going to exotic places, doing mysterious things, risking life and personal honor to keep the Big Dominos from dropping. I didn't foresee spending the rest of my life immured in the Harvard and MIT libraries, translating and summarizing Soviet journals and magazines. Soviet academese is just as opaque and boring as the American variety, and their journalism makes *U.S. News & World Report* look positively effervescent.

So when we do find an actual spy, everybody in the section gets somewhat wired. It would have been fun just to keep watching him, maybe push him a little bit, but we don't really have any autonomy in such matters. We had to send a report to the Foreign Resources Division at Langley, and they sent back the expected reply: Wait.

It turned out to be a fruitful wait, though. A couple of months later I got a padded envelope through Federal Express. It contained one sheet of paper, which was just what we needed to make Nicholas Foley turn.

His office hours at MIT were from ten to twelve on Tuesdays and Wednesdays, we knew. I went to meet him at noon on Tuesday.

The door was wide open, Foley engrossed in a book, feet up on his desk. The wall that wasn't solid books had dozens of framed watercolors, which I knew were his wife's work. (I had earlier come upon the interesting and not-too-odd coincidence that she and I had studied watercolors with the same person, five years apart, at the Cambridge Adult Education Center. She was better than I.) The place looked lived-in but scrupulously neat.

He didn't look too much like the file photo, which was a two-year-old candid shot of him mowing the lawn. With his professor's uniform—shapeless corduroy suit—he was impressive in a bearish, avuncular way. He was a big man with a paunch, but he moved with grace and precision. Unfashionably long hair, blond shot through with white, and a silky full beard.

"Dr. Foley," I said, "sorry to barge in on you like

this, but we have a student in common, a woman I'm having a problem with. Could we talk?" I dropped a note in front of him that said, "Let's talk outside," in Russian.

He stared at the note for a moment and then looked at me over his bifocals. "Of course. Are you free for lunch?" He rolled the note into a tiny ball as we agreed on a restaurant, and dropped it into his pocket.

Neither of us said anything further until we were out of the building, walking toward Kendall Square. When he spoke, I could hardly hear his whispered Russian over the traffic noise: "—This is a first. Is it something urgent?"

"Possibly. Interesting, at any rate." I guided him toward a bus-stop bench and asked him to sit. Then I opened the padded envelope and handed it to him.

His expression never changed. He glanced at the short document, looked at me once, and then reread it.

Under an NKVD letterhead, typed in uneven Cyrillic capitals: "SPIES AND COLLABORATORS EXECUTED IN MONTH OF DECEMBER 1941" followed by a list of thirty-four names. There was a red circle around the names of his mother and father.

He put it back in the envelope and returned it to me. "You aren't who I thought you were."

"No," I said. "State Department."

He smiled wryly at that. "Sure. State." After a moment: "So what are you going to do?"

"The next move is yours, actually." I sat down next to him; the plastic windbreak gave us a pocket of privacy on the busy sidewalk. "You are an agent for the KGB. I've just shown you proof that they killed your parents. So?"

He smiled and took off his glasses and started to

polish them with a handkerchief. "What is your name?"

"You can call me Jake or Jacob."

"Jacob. Thank you. Let me see." He put the glasses back on and blinked at me with an unreadable expression. "I'm trying to gather my thoughts. This is rather much to absorb."

"Take your time."

"Yes. Thank you." He stared intently at the wind sculpture over the subway entrance. "Let me first dispose of the obvious. Anyone can find an old typewriter with Cyrillic characters—in Boston, anyhow. And the CIA—I mean the 'State Department'—is no doubt capable of printing stationery with an NKVD seal."

"I can assure you that—"

"No." He held up a finger, still staring across the street. "I'm not saying I disbelieve you. Not about the document. Just acknowledging technicalities, for my own . . . predisposition toward completeness.

"Second, more important. This document is most of a half century old. I hope you don't take it as a lack of filial piety if I tell you that I am not greatly moved by it. Nor surprised." He shifted around to look squarely at me. "I am no fool, Jacob. I've studied this period with some intensity; Soviet and German sources as well as American. No . . . what would *surprise* me would be proof that my parents had survived. For thirty years or more I've known that if they had somehow lived through the siege of Leningrad, they would have been killed during the Stalinist purges."

"You know this, and yet you work for them?"

"The Stalinists?" He smiled ironically. "In the beginning there was the Cheka. The Cheka begat the OGPU. The OGPU begat the NKVD, which begat the NKGB, which begat the MGB, which begat the KGB. Actually, it's more complicated than that. But you get my point. The KGB is not the organization that arrested and executed my parents."

"It is their successor."

"To about the same degree that your CIA is the successor to the Tory spies of King George. Things have changed rapidly in Russia since the War."

Two arguing women stepped in front of us to wait for the bus. I gestured, and we both got up and walked on down the street. We fell in behind a man walking a fast Doberman and let him stride out of earshot.

"I'm flattered that you've gone to such evident trouble over me," he said, "but I'm also puzzled. You must know that I'm not actually a KGB agent."

I managed not to laugh. "Really."

"Not in any real sense. Tell me, what have I done that you could take to a court of law?"

"If I told you, I'd be compromising my sources," I said. This wasn't going according to plan. "But do you deny that you were born in Russia, trained by the MGB in a Soviet camp called Rivertown, and illegally inserted into this country with false documents? Do you?"

"In 1953 I did immigrate here without proper papers. I was a child, though."

"It's still straight out of James Bond. I'm not worried about being able to prove you're a spy. Coffee?"

"Sure." We stepped into a crowded café, the one we had mentioned in his office, and found an isolated table in the back.

I pressed him further. "Look. All I have to do is pick up the phone and call the FBI. They won't even give you time to pack. You'll be deported by Thursday."

"Perhaps."

"We don't like to do things that way. The FBI's way. You'd be replaced, and it might take us years to track down your replacement. We'd much rather make an arrangement with you."

"Turn me into a counterspy." He said it with droll gravity. "A Double . . . Agent."

"In essence. Just keep us informed; make monthly reports as to your activities."

He smiled. "They would be short reports. If you've done your job at all well, you must know that." He was quiet while the waitress poured our coffee. "I'm not sure what I know that would be of the slightest interest to you. The only spy I know by name is named Jacob."

My father, who's a union negotiator, taught me that sometimes the best way to get someone to make a concession is to remain silent. Let the other man open his mouth and hope that he traps himself. Someone must have taught Foley that, too. For about a minute we looked at each other, sipping coffee.

Finally he leaned back in his chair and looked up to his right. That either meant he was about to tell the truth or he knew that people who are about to lie tend to look left. He spoke softly.

"I've sometimes wondered how it is in real life. With spies, I mean. Suppose I said all right, I'll go along with what you want, and then I go straight to my KGB contact and tell him or her what's happened. So he or she gives me false information to pass on to you. And so maybe I turn around and tell *you*. Or maybe I'm feeding you some prefabricated line. How can either you or the KGB contact trust anything I tell you?"

"We have ways of checking," I said. "Besides, we

can punish you for lying. Throw you in jail or deport you."

He nodded. "I still don't think I've done anything you could jail me for. And as for deportation ... I suspect the Soviets would treat me well, allow me to continue my research."

"And your wife? She would go with you?"

He hesitated just a moment too long. "Yes. I have no doubt."

"Well, you may have the opportunity to find out very soon. Unless you cooperate."

"Yes, of course." He frowned. "I have to think. You've been fairly open with me, Jacob; I'll return the favor. My first impulse is to say the hell with it and let you deport me—while I'm still not in any serious trouble with you or the KGB. You must see the logic of that."

I had to admit that I did. "There are a few problems with that course, though," he continued. "Mainly Valerie. She'd have to learn Russian, the life as well as the language. Very difficult. Also, although I suppose I'm technically a Soviet citizen, I grew up an American and am used to this life. Attached to it.

"Finally, it has belatedly occurred to me that you may not be what you say. You could be a KGB agent investigating my loyalty. The only way I can really test your identity is to force you into some overt action. Like having me deported."

"No, I can prove that I am who I claim to be."

"Of course you can—but would that finally prove anything? By your own testimony, the fact that you work for the CIA doesn't mean you don't also work for the KGB. Right? And maybe the British and Belgian and Bolivian secret services as well." He laughed. "What a complicated world you must inhabit."

"No, wait. You're setting up a zero-sum game for yourself. The only way you'll trust me is for me to perform an act that takes you out of the picture? That doesn't make any sense."

"On the contrary, it makes a great deal of sense, if my primary motivation is to protect my own skin. Suppose you *were* a double agent, and I agreed to turn against the KGB. Wouldn't some assassin with a silenced Uzi come after me?"

"That's ridiculous."

"You're right. They'd make it look like an accident; push me onto the subway tracks."

"Come on."

"Inject me with a tiny bead of radioactive thallium. From an umbrella."

I paused at that. "You must know better."

"They did that once, didn't they? I should say 'we.' That's what the newspapers said."

"Not here. The Soviets haven't killed an American since 1941, at least not on American soil."

"Ah." He was suddenly serious. "But I'm not an American." He stood up abruptly. "As I say, I have to think. Perhaps I have to screw up my courage and discuss it with Valerie."

"I could give you a day. Don't discuss—"

"Two days. I'll meet you here at noon on Thursday." He turned and started to walk out, then came back and put two quarters by his cup. "See you Thursday."

Our tail, Roberta Bender, had been nursing a beer at the counter. She walked out just in front of him. I waited for a few minutes to see whether there might have been another tail, a KGB one, but no one else left the diner immediately. Maybe they followed *me* out.

I remembered feeling apprehensive lest he try something suspicious. I didn't want to lose him; he seemed like a good man, and I felt that working with him would be interesting.

It was going to be more than interesting. Terrifying.

CHAPTER FOUR

NICK

THE FIRST TIME I used it to kill somebody, it was almost an accident. A mugger.

For nearly five years now, I've been wearing a miniaturized signal generator built into my wristwatch, which I "convinced" one of my more gifted students to cobble together for me. I used it a few times, trivially, to make sure it worked, and then more or less forgot about it. I didn't want to get in the habit of using it for trivial things.

I try to keep my weight down, without dramatic success, by relying on a bicycle for transportation as much as possible. That was how I managed to run into a mugger.

There'd been a reception for a guest speaker at the Institute, and it was almost eleven when I got on my bike and headed home. About halfway, the thing gave a crunch and a lurch and the back wheel locked up. In the dim streetlight I could just discern what had happened: The rear derailleur had slipped off its mount and gotten wedged in between the spokes and the frame. The bike was going no farther that night. I locked it to the nearest parking meter and started walking home. (The nearest T stop was almost as far away as my flat off Central Square.) I followed the advice of all the newspaper articles and walked briskly, looking straight ahead, right hand in my jacket pocket. Wrapped around the deadly granola bar I'd forgotten was there.

He wasn't dressed like a hood and he wasn't black, and his eyes didn't burn with junkie fire. He was probably working his way through college.

He stepped out of a doorway and presented an effective argument: a long-barreled .44 Magnum revolver *à la* the Clint Eastwood folk hero. "Give me your wallet," he said, an unnecessary refinement.

I had my hands in the air and was about to tell him that the wallet was in my inside coat pocket—obviously, I didn't want to reach for it—when he said, "The watch, too."

I reached for the watch and pushed the button. I took a step toward him.

"Stay there." He hauled back on the hammer, cocking it with two clicks: soft, loud. "I'm not fucking around."

"Take the pistol," I said, "put the muzzle in your mouth, and pull the trigger."

He shook his head slowly and whispered, "No." Then he put the muzzle in his mouth and pulled the trigger.

The report was so loud it stung my face like a slap. The bullet shattered the glass transom of the shoe store behind him, setting off the burglar alarm, and spraying the entrance alcove with blood and brains and chips of bone. The pistol clattered to the sidewalk, and he took one lurching step toward me, curious slack expression on his face, and then folded up like an abandoned marionette. His legs twitched as if he were trying to run away. Blood geysered from an artery embedded in the fist-sized exit wound. I watched the fountain slow to a trickle. Smiling.

After forty years I had returned to the territory of my childhood. But this time the one suddenly beyond help, suddenly meat, was not a friend or relative or fellow traveler—but someone who deserved it. Who had asked for it and got it. I recognized the grisly elated feeling, a very specific memory: In the spring, after the siege had lifted, we were playing in the forest outside of the city and came upon the dry old corpse of a Nazi soldier. My older friend, Yuri, had a camp ax, actually a small, blunt hatchet, and we took turns hacking away at the weathered remains. Laughing like a family of hyena cubs. Finally rolling around in the mud helpless with gleeful horror. Over the next few months we combed the woods carefully, repeating the experience many times. The Nazis had left in a hurry, no time to bury all their dead.

A police car screeched to a stop at the curb. I didn't turn around, but could see the drama reflected in the glass of the shoe store's display window. The driver piled out of the car and took refuge behind its hood, his pistol in a two-handed grip aligned steadily on me. I thought it prudent to raise my hands. The other officer swarmed out of the passenger seat into a rather vulnerable kneeling position, with a riot gun aimed at the small of my back. They were shouting simultaneously, very hard to understand with the siren going *wow-wow-wow,* but the gist of it was clear. I was not to move or try anything funny. I was to keep my hands, my fucking hands, in the air and turn to face them, slowly. I obeyed.

The driver rushed around the car's hood and put the muzzle of his gun under my chin while he patted me in the obvious places. The other one played a flashlight beam on the remains of the mugger and then bolted for the curb and vomited.

The driver walked me roughly toward the corpse and pinned me up against the glass. I could hear his sharp gasp as he surveyed the damage.

"What the *fuck*. Point-blank in the mouth. Drug deal?"

"No, it was suicide." No harm in approximating the truth. "He started to mug me and then turned his weapon on himself."

"Yeah. And I'm Mary Tyler Moore."

"It's true. The pistol should be somewhere near him on the ground."

His partner turned off the siren and returned, smelling of gastric juices. "Let's get an ID."

"Yeah. Who are you?"

"Miranda," his partner said tightly.

"That's right. You have the right to remain silent—"

"No, that's okay," I said, assuming the watch would work without the siren's interference. "Trust me. Put your weapons down." They did, and I lowered my hands. "Did either of you gentlemen mention me on the radio?"

They looked at each other. "No," the driver said, "we didn't know you was here until the headlights picked you up."

"All right. Then just forget you ever saw me." They nodded seriously. "Oh. There's a disabled bicycle locked to a parking meter a couple of blocks away. You will not connect that in any way with this incident." They both nodded again. I walked away, ducking down a side street just in time to avoid being seen by the Rescue Squad ambulance.

That night I had complicated dreams, but then woke feeling purged. Two weeks later I did it again. Valerie was out of town, so I went down to the Combat Zone and made myself conspicuous well after midnight. "Trolling for trouble" was the phrase that occurred to me. I killed a pimp and a mugger in ways that appeared to be suicide and accident.

It became a sort of ongoing hobby. I stopped counting after the thirteenth, for luck.

I went back to the office after talking to the spy Jacob and spent most of the afternoon attempting to refine a computer model that was supposed to relate various demographic and personality factors to seven distinct patterns of language-acquisition resistance. It was a waste of several hours; my mind kept wandering. I was really just putting off going home. Valerie doesn't go to school on Tuesdays, and I neither wanted to rush home and confess that I happened to be a spy for the Evil Empire nor sit around the house and stew about it. So I went home at the usual hour and we followed the usual routine: a drink and a chat before I prepared dinner (simple *carbonara* and salad), then eat and retire, Valerie to her drawing board and me to the "library," an extra bedroom full of books and journals. I poured a glass of brandy and lit a cigar, I suppose as an unconscious signal.

Valerie tapped on the door, opened it, and leaned on the jamb. "All right," she said, "what's bugging you?"

It's interesting how a man can be articulate and even eloquent in front of a classroom and yet be reduced to tongue-tied confusion when confronted by the woman he lives with and loves. "Uh," I said and completed the thought with a spastic gesture.

"The last time you smoked during the week was when they threatened to make you department head. The time before that was your little under*grad*uate. You've also been as sociable as a grumpy reptile. So what is it this time?"

"Not an undergraduate."

"Moving up in the world?"

"Not sex at all. Nor office politics." I sighed and patted the seat next to me. "It *is* politics, though. Sit down. It's a long story."

She listened without comment for a good half hour, while I told her the truth about Leningrad and Rivertown and Iowa and my subsequent twenty-year career as a semispy. I did not mention the wristwatch hypnotic device or the free-lance social work to which I applied it. I told her about Jacob.

"This is all true?" she said finally.

"Yes. I'm sorry." To that she laughed nervously and took a sip of my brandy. Then she stood up and went over to look out the window.

"I just don't know what to say. I understand? Is that what I'm supposed to say?"

"I'm—"

"Please don't say you're sorry again." She turned and sat back against the window ledge. "Look. I've known for almost two years that something strange was going on. I found your gun, the one with the shoulder holster. I didn't think it was for coaching the pistol club."

I met her stare but didn't say anything. She looked down at the floor. "I was ashamed about snooping, I guess, and . . . I mean, who could *imagine*? I thought it was just a piece of male silliness, like those knives. I mean, you're such a calm and rational guy." A tear started. "So mild and . . . sweet—"

"Sounds like a cigarette ad," I said. "Firm and fully packed?" She laughed and dabbed at her eyes with a knuckle.

"*I'm* the left-wing nut of the family," she said. "You're not even political."

"No, I'm very political. Have to hide it, of course."

She shook her head, nibbling her lower lip. "But the gun. You say you don't do that kind of spy stuff."

"I suppose it is about ninety percent macho aberration. I told myself I had to be prepared for any eventuality." I let a little truth leak through: "My childhood, the terrors, that's all very close to the surface even now. The world is a dangerous place, full of sudden, random death. Even for law-abiding citizens. Like me."

"You choose the laws you want to abide by, though."

"Like everyone," we said simultaneously, and then laughed.

"This is a hell of a forty-fifth birthday present," she said, smiling. "Learn Russian at my age?"

"You would go?"

She looked at me for a long time, perhaps parsing out a dramatic reply. Finally she just nodded, hard, and began silently crying. I held her for a long time. We changed venue, to the bedroom, and had some fine, slow hours.

CHAPTER FIVE

JACOB

FOR MORE THAN a year we've had a listening device in Nicholas Foley's library (and living room and bedroom). It finally paid off in a small way. A negative way. We know we can't play his wife against him.

Something has come up that rather complicates the Foley situation. It may not be important at all, but we all have a "feeling."

The first hint of it was his mail. His journals. Twenty years ago he had a brief flirtation with hypnosis and even published one paper on the subject. Then he apparently dropped it completely; at least he's never done any formal work in it again. Yet he not only still subscribes to the hypnosis journals he took back then, but he also picked up the subscriptions to two new journals that started in the seventies and eighties.

Maybe nothing more than a hobby; his department doesn't pay for the subscriptions. But it's not the only thing that's a bit odd. In the course of an interview, without any coaching, one of his student subjects related a strange incident: Twice Foley asked him to do absurd things that had nothing to do with the business at hand—one time it was to whistle "Silent Night" (in July) and the other was to pretend to be riding a bicycle. On a third occasion Foley asked him to go back to the dorm and fetch a particular pencil. He refused; Foley claimed to have been misunderstood. He was not asked back.

Those do sound like the sort of things that stage hypnotists use to demonstrate their skills. Maybe he was innocently experimenting with the monotony that accompanies foreign-language vocabulary lessons— that was the context, which is why it surprised the student enough for him to have remembered it twelve years later—but if that were the case, why didn't he simply tell the subject why he had made the request, rather than try to misdirect him?

I wished we could have transcripts for the past year's bugs, to see whether anything about hypnosis had come up between Foley and his wife, but of course there was no budget for that. I fast-ran through several days' tapes, but there was no hint of anything in that direction. They did work together with it a long time ago, before they were married. But a check of her office bookshelves at Boston University reveals nothing interesting. Within a day or two we should have a listing of all the books she has checked out of the university's library since it's been computerized. I don't expect any surprises. (There were no real surprises in the list of Foley's borrowings we got from the MIT library computer system.) You can never tell, though.

Computers are a boon to this business. More lists.

Foley was waiting for me at the diner, finishing what appeared to be a Bloody Mary. I was perversely certain there was no alcohol in it; at any rate, I'm not a good quarry for that particular trap. One drink and

I'm halfway to dreamland. I sat down and signaled for coffee.

We exchanged greetings. "You've decided?" I asked.

"Yes, pretty much." He also righted his cup, and neither of us said anything while the waitress served us coffee and thimbles of ersatz milk and the phrase "witcha 'n minnit."

"My wife and I discussed the alternatives. We decided the best thing would be to wave a magic wand and make you disappear."

That gave me a premonitory shiver. "Meaning?"

"We've decided not to decide, not yet. We both need more time to weigh it."

This had not been on the tape. "How long?"

"Nine days." He blew on his coffee and stared at me over the top, through the steam.

"That's too long . . . why so specific?"

"Business trip. To Paris."

"Out of the question." He checked his watch, an odd gesture. "You have to decide sooner—and no matter what your decision, we can't let you out of the country."

"Why not? If I turn out to be a bad guy, you'll be deporting me anyhow." That did make a certain amount of sense. "Why not just send somebody along to keep an eye on me? Why not come yourself?"

"I'd enjoy that," I said. "I haven't been to France in years."

"Would the Agency pay for it?"

"I can put in a request, but I doubt they'll honor it."

He nodded. "Well, you could come on your own. Make a holiday of it." The waitress came then and took our orders. Then, I swear, we started chatting about various places we'd been in Paris, what it would be like this time of year, what his linguistics conference would be like, and what his paper was going to be about—with neither he nor I questioning that we were both going there next week.

After listening to the conversation several times (I had a small tape recorder in my pocket) I'm forced to admit that he did somehow hypnotize me—or in some mild way bring me under his control. He's a persuasive man, and earnest and friendly, but certainly not what you would call charismatic. It wasn't the strength of his personality that kept me from bringing up the unpleasant business of what-we-can-do-to-you-if-you-don't-cooperate. He did something. Next time I'll be on the lookout, catch him at it. Probably some sort of parlor-trick thing; I'll have to read up on hypnosis.

There were still a few spaces left on the cheap open-seating flight to Paris that Foley will be taking. I bought a ticket just in case. Maybe I just wanted to see Paris one more time before I die.

CHAPTER SIX

NICK

THAT WAS A risky session with Jacob. I had to be circumspect, assuming that we were being recorded, and not give him any direct, unambiguous orders. But I think it worked. At least several days have gone by and I haven't yet been arrested, Uzi'd, or pushed beneath a subway train.

I got a memo through interoffice mail, presumably from the KGB, arranging for a rendezvous on Saturday with "Lynn." He or she was to meet me at two in the afternoon outside the Harvard Square Theater in Cambridge. That would be difficult, since I'd be in Paris. Of course there's no way I could get in touch with them—other than going down to the Soviet embassy in Washington, which I have always assumed was against the rules. I put a prominent note on my office door saying I would be out of town from the ninth through the thirteenth and hoped the news would get to them.

I shouldn't have worried. The day before the trip I was hunched over my bicycle, fighting the Kryptonite lock, when a familiar voice behind me said, "So you're going to Paris, Nikola?"

I hadn't seen Lubinov in almost two years, and I

greeted him with honest warmth. We walked and traded politenesses for a minute while my brain ground through the various possibilities, and finally I decided there was only one safe course.

"Vladimir, there's a real problem. I may . . . no longer be useful." He just looked at me, expressionless. "I've been approached by the CIA. They know I have KGB contacts and want me to be a double agent. They've threatened me with deportation."

He squeezed my shoulder and actually smiled. "I'm glad you told me this. Cooperate with them, at least for the time being. Try to gain their confidence."

"You knew?"

He shrugged. "Let me not say. What hotel are you occupying in Paris?" I told him. "Good. We may have people there who want to be, would want, *will* want to talk to you. My English," he said, smiling.

"Much improved," I said. Actually, it seemed about the same as ever, which was odd. He'd been in the country longer than I.

"Yes, of course. And your French? If our representatives must use it?"

"My French is good. I could probably struggle along in Russian if I had to."

"I should not think," he said, and stopped. "Well. I will see you next time." We said good-bye, and he walked briskly down Main Street.

I crossed over to Legal Seafood and sat in the noisy bar nursing an expensive beer, trying to reason things out. Did the KGB have a contact in Jacob's group? I would have to act as if it were so. Should I take the playing-both-ends-against-the-middle game one step further and tell Jacob? No. Not yet—

And whose side am I on? Besides my own, and Valerie's?

Could Jacob himself be the double agent? The note

on my door didn't say Paris, but Vladimir knew. Because Jacob knew?

Too paranoiac. Vladimir could have called MIT; the departmental secretary knows where I'm going and would have no reason not to tell anybody who asked.

Still, "tightrope" is more than a metaphor for this situation. I must proceed with extreme care.

I turned on the watch as we approached the security stop on the way to our flight. I took the lead-lined bag out of my carry-on luggage and handed it to the attendant. "Just a camera and film," I said.

She looked in the bag at the camera and film and nine-millimeter automatic. She nodded and handed it back. I kept the watch generator running as we walked to the International Departures Waiting Lounge. Hot and stuffy; smell of European cigarettes.

We found two isolated seats together. Ninety minutes, plenty of time. When Jacob sat down, I handed him a notebook. "Read this," I said.

On the first page of the notebook I'd printed:

1. SAY, "THIS IS INTERESTING."
2. WRITE DOWN EVERYTHING THE CIA KNOWS OR SUSPECTS ABOUT ME.
3. WHEN YOU ARE DONE WRITING, HAND ME THE NOTEBOOK AND FORGET EVERYTHING ABOUT IT. YOU WILL REMEMBER HAVING NAPPED FOR THE PAST HOUR.

"This is interesting," he said. Then he turned the page and started writing. I had to hope we weren't being watched, a reasonable risk for the return. I did assume that the conversation was going on tape, but hoped that silence wouldn't be too suspicious. While he was writing, I started the horror novel that Valerie said would keep my mind off the flight. It was so absorbing that I jumped when, an hour later, Jacob touched me with the edge of the notebook.

I took it, and he rubbed his eyes. "Must have dropped off."

"It's awfully warm. Up late last night?"

"Oh yeah. Last-minute details."

I turned on the watch again. "You'll want to sleep on the plane, then." He nodded. We talked amiably until our flight was called, then we filed into the 747, and in the process of buckling up he began to snore.

He had written four fascinating pages. Not surprisingly, in some matters the CIA knew more about my life than I did myself—for instance, the actual name of my KGB primary contact is Vladimir *Borachev;* he's a market analyst for the Soviet trade mission in New York City. My wife's dossier from the sixties includes suspicion of complicity in burning down an ROTC building; she didn't go to trial, but that may have been because she was sleeping with the FBI informer.

Of my own amorous excesses he only notes the ones that Valerie is aware of, so they're probably the result of our apartment being bugged (she does occasionally refer aloud to my checkered past). There is no suspicion of my Social-Darwinism-with-a-gun hobby, or infirmity.

They are on the track of my device, though, at least to the extent of making a connection with hypnotism. A woman who interviewed my test subjects noted that two of them remembered my asking them to do ridiculous things, and they both were dropped from the study soon afterward. She correctly interpreted this as a test of hypnotic technique. Jacob has added his own suspicions.

I read the four pages over again, with mounting despair. There was no going back; no matter what happened, our comfortable life in Cambridge was over. We were going to be compelled either to move to the Soviet Union or to drop out of sight in the "Free" World, eventually to emerge with new identities.

Of course I had given this some thought before. With new identities in the West, neither of us could practice our true professions, and we would go through life perpetually looking over our shoulders, being suspicious of everyone—which would also be true in the Soviet Union, to some extent. But at least in the USSR we wouldn't have to pretend to be something we weren't. And I could probably continue my researches, even if Valerie was not allowed to. Abnormal psychology is rather a different line of work in the Soviet Union.

I spent much of the flight thinking about the options within those two limited options. On the Soviet side, Valerie could possibly wind up with an interesting job in intelligence—nothing requiring high security clearance, of course, but something that would take advantage of her being a natural-born American. I remembered my teachers at Rivertown and wondered how many of them were recycled spies or relatives of spies. She might perversely enjoy the work. Or she might have a belated attack of patriotism.

Of course we weren't limited to the United States if we decided not to go to the Soviet Union. We could obtain citizenship papers wherever we wished to go; my watch is better than any passport. Valerie can get along in French and Spanish, and with our savings we could live fairly well in Spain or Mexico or on some

Caribbean island. I entertained that fantasy for a few minutes before realizing that wherever we wound up, we couldn't afford to be conspicuous. Not with both the KGB and the CIA after us. So we probably had best not stray from the States or Canada.

North America's a big place, though. By the time the plane landed, I'd made my decision. Unless Valerie was dead set against it, we'd just pull up stakes and start over in the United States. Screw the CIA, the KGB, the FBI, the American Association of Psychologists. We'd find something.

Having slept all the way, Jacob was ready to kick up his heels. He'd been to Paris only once for a few days as a student, and working for the CIA (popular conceptions to the contrary) restricted rather than expanded his opportunities for foreign travel. But I was exhausted; once we'd cleared Customs and found the hotel, and all I wanted was sleep. This presented an obvious dilemma, since he was not supposed to let me out of his sight. I turned on my watch and told him it was all right: I'd stay put; he could go out and enjoy himself. I hoped for his own sake his enthusiasm wasn't being recorded.

(I suppose I should know more about these things. Could he be wired up with a recorder and yet not trigger the airport search alarm? Maybe it was in his briefcase, disguised as a tuna fish sandwich. Maybe it was implanted in his skull.)

So I put up my feet and went over the paper I was going to deliver, hoping that its familiarity would put me to sleep. Perversely, it stimulated me into wakefulness. I wandered out to a *magasin* store and chose some good bread, cheese, and wine to keep in the room. My French did not meet with the merchant's approval, but he did manage to find all the proper items.

I tried to summon up enthusiasm for being in Paris again, but it was rush hour; murderous traffic and poisonous air; so after walking around the block deciding not to do this and not to do that, I just picked up a newspaper and retreated to the room, and found it had been searched by an amateur.

Well, perhaps only by someone who didn't care whether the search was discovered—or wanted me or Jacob to discover it, as a warning. I had aligned the typed page I was reading exactly along the first line of the page beneath it, an elementary precaution. The person who went through the pages had simply stacked them afterward and had not even put them back in quite the same position, squared with the corner of the table's blotter. I wondered whether he'd found what he was after; he couldn't have had more than ten or twelve minutes, even with a lookout posted downstairs to say, "Go."

The lead bag with the gun was where I had hidden it, out of sight on top of the old-fashioned toilet tank. From now on I would take it with me when I left the room.

American, Russian, or French? Checking up on me, or Jacob? It could have been Jacob himself, actually, waiting for me to leave and then doubling back. But in that case I should think he'd be more likely to follow me. Rather than read through a speech he could see for the asking. I decided not to waste time worrying about it. Opened the box of dime-store Burgundy and drank off a fast, sour tumbler of it. They hadn't had wine in boxes the last time I was in France, and with luck they won't have them the next time. Then I stretched out in the semidarkness and told my toes to relax, then ankles, shins, and so forth; old autohypnosis routine for falling asleep. Just as I reached the chin, which normally does it, a key rattled in the door, and it creaked open. "Jacob?"

"*Nyet.*" I looked up, and there were two men in honest-to-God trench coats standing in the doorway. "Please, light?"

"Sure." I switched on the light by the bed. "—Would you have wine?" I said in Russian, sitting up. "—It's nothing extraordinary . . ."

"—Thank you, no. Come with us." It took me a moment to place his accent: Bulgarian. That was a bad sign. You don't have to know much about the trade to know who does wet work for the KGB in Europe.

I started to get my jacket. "—Not necessary. We're not going outside." They were a real Mutt-and-Jeff team. The one who was doing all the talking was a tall, blond, handsome fellow with a fixed, intense expression. Like the TV Russian spy who gave me so much secret amusement on *The Man from U.N.C.L.E.* in my youth. His partner, from another division of Central Casting, was short and swarthy, with organ-grinder mustaches, carrying a large, shabby briefcase. He seemed to be concentrating on something else.

I turned on the watch and tried to think of some test that would be innocuous, in case we were being monitored. "—Do have a glass of wine while I use the bathroom." This time they both nodded, and I poured two tumblers. Fairly strong evidence, if not really conclusive. I'd tested the machine on foreign students and American students speaking second languages, but never on a Bulgarian who was speaking Russian.

In the bathroom I considered the pistol. It would look pretty obvious stuck under my shirt; I decided to do without. I replaced it over the tank and waited for a biologically reasonable length of time, then flushed the toilet.

They looked odd, standing there in trench coats with their water glasses of wine, their serious expressions. "—Did you search my room earlier?" I asked.

Jeff, the tall one, shook his head slowly. "—Search room?"

"—Guess I was mistaken." I turned off the watch. "—Shall we go?"

The room they'd rented was obviously the cheapest available, a one-bed closet with bathroom down the hall. They evidently hadn't seen it before; Mutt grumbled something in Bulgarian about the expense for how small it was. We had to do a kind of dance while they took off their trench coats.

"—Please sit." There was only the bed and a hard chair. Jeff sat in the chair, after reversing it so he could prop his forearms on the back. The bed made a rusty squeak when I eased myself onto it. Mutt leaned against the door, looking lethal with an obvious shoulder-holster bulge. They both had an almost neutral, vaguely hostile stare. Probably part of the Bulgarian KGB uniform. Neither of them said anything for a long moment.

"—Who are you?" I said as a sort of icebreaker.

"—That is none of your concern." He waited a long time, stroking his chin in a stylized gesture of thinking, then almost shouted. "—You are here with an agent of the American CIA."

"—Yes, of course. This has been reported to my KGB section chief in America."

Mutt addressed me for the first time. "—We know nothing of this."

"—Is that true?" Jeff didn't answer. He just stared. He was starting to annoy me. "—Then I suggest we go no further until you have had a chance to confer with your superiors." I started to get up.

"—Sit!" they both said. "—We have no superiors here," Jeff said. "—Does this CIA man know of your connection with the KGB?"

"—He does. He's trying to recruit me as a double agent. I'm supposed to go along with it, to a point."

"—So he takes you to Paris with him," Mutt said.

"—It's the other way around. I'm here on legitimate business, academic business. He's tagging along to make sure I don't defect." Mutt nodded wisely at that, as if I couldn't "defect" from the United States by buying a plane ticket out, but Jeff frowned.

"—Please do not joke with us. You claim that this man knows you are a KGB agent and yet he allows you to go to a foreign country, to be alone in a foreign country?"

"—That's correct."

"—It seems fantastic."

"—I don't believe him," Mutt said. "—There is more to this. Otherwise we wouldn't have been alerted."

"—So go to the people who alerted you and ask for more information. I'm not going anywhere."

"—Indeed you are not." Mutt opened his briefcase and brought out a coil of about five yards of clothesline. "—Get in the chair."

"—That's not necessary," I said.

Jeff stood up. "—I think perhaps it is. At least for now. We'll be back by evening."

"—I refuse."

"—You may not," Mutt said, smiling as he unbuttoned his jacket to expose the automatic pistol.

That was enough. I turned on the watch. "—Do you have a gun, too?" I asked Jeff.

"—No. Dobri's is enough."

"—Put on your coats. We're going for a walk." I got my own coat, and we walked to the nearest Metro stop. I escorted them to Gare Nord and put them on the first train out to nowhere—to Hautmont, actually, that being as far as their money would carry them, while staying within the French borders. I gave them specific instructions as to what to do when they got there and then returned to the hotel. Jacob was waiting in the room.

"I was worried about you. Where have you been?"

"Met a couple of friends." I turned on the watch. "Let's go down and get a drink." We went to the noisy bar downstairs, and I told him what to do: first, let me have that nice diplomatic passport. Now, here's five thousand francs. Live it up; stay drunk for at least three days. When you sober up, you will remember absolutely nothing about me.

Bridges burned, I picked up some more money on the way out to Orly. I used the diplomatic papers and my watch to rush through Customs and on to a waiting Concorde. In the air less than three hours after I'd put Mutt and Jeff aboard the train, I was sure I'd be home long before the shit hit the fan. I was wrong.

CHAPTER SEVEN

NICK

WE DROVE OUT of Cambridge through increasingly heavy snow, but luckily it abated somewhat in an hour. Richard, the boy I'd abducted, was a good, careful driver, and his van had snow tires. We were able to maintain a steady forty-five miles per hour until about midnight. When he started to yawn and blink, I suggested that we take the next exit and nap for a bit. I didn't feel I had enough driving experience to take over the wheel in this weather.

I let him sleep for ninety minutes while I read newspapers and drank coffee in an all-night truck stop. Certainly not enough rest for the boy, but I was nervous. It wasn't likely we were being followed, having been off the interstate since the New Hampshire border, but I didn't want to press my luck.

Some years ago an IRA terrorist told Margaret Thatcher, "We only have to be lucky once. You have to be lucky all the time." That's the way I was starting to feel. The KGB would have only limited resources for tracking me down in this country. But as soon as Jacob woke up hung over in a Parisian drunk tank and claimed diplomatic immunity, the real hunt would be on. I wanted to be well camouflaged before the FBI blew the whistle.

I got two very large coffees to go, went out to the van, and shook Richard awake. His body didn't want to cooperate, so I gave him the "suggestion" that he had just had eight hours of sleep and was full of energy. It worked, but of course it's not something to be used too often. He chattered incessantly all the way to Bangor, Maine.

All I knew about Maine I learned from Stephen King novels, so it seemed a rather foreboding place. Bangor especially, with all the brooding, large Victorian houses, stark and seeming uninhabited in the early-morning snowscape. But it was a town well suited to my purposes and perhaps to my current mood as well.

If I were totally amoral, I would have taken the easiest and most prudent course and eliminated Richard. Bangor had a convenient river. Instead, I told him to drive to California, taking at least a week. Credit cards were out of the question, of course, so I had to go to a bank and ask for a couple of thousand in used twenties. Then I had to rent him a car (try doing *that* without a credit card!) and take care of his van. I told him to return the car in Los Angeles and then take the bus to Las Vegas; then fly back to Boston and phone home from the airport, remembering nothing since the night he walked into the Greek bar. They might just possibly link me with a convenient amnesia victim, but there was no way they could follow the trail back to Bangor. Especially since I arranged for his van to be parked on a side street in upstate New York.

I began to put into motion a plan whose details I had been mulling over for several years. The greatest danger I faced was being recognized from a distance, too great a distance for the device to work. So I started a program that would radically and permanently change my physical appearance.

First I shaved off my beard, then cut my sixties-style long hair down to a crew and bleached it. I traded in my bifocals for blue-tinted contact lenses (which I had been carrying and using in secret for some years), and bought a shabby working-man's wardrobe at Goodwill. Sunlamp for an outdoorsy look. Then I set about losing some of the fifty pounds of fat I'd collected at Cambridge. Fasting on fruit juice, vitamins, and phenylalanine, with some light exercise.

In a month or so I would be ready to head for Washington. Or Langley, Virginia, actually.

CHAPTER EIGHT

VALERIE

I HAD MY arms full of groceries, the bags ready to spill, finally got both locks open, and stumbled into the apartment, and this big guy grabbed me from behind, I mean really crushed me, one leather-gloved hand over my mouth and big arm pinning me to his chest, groceries and all; door kicked shut behind me and he whispered, *"One sound and you die,"* with a thick accent, only thing either of them ever said in English.

Started to struggle and he crushed me twice as tightly; moved his hand up to pinch off my nose. Suffocating, I nodded, and he eased off. A bald man stepped in front of me and pointed a gun at my heart, one of those little machine-gun pistols the bad guys always have on television. The other one took my grocery bags, one in each paw, and carried them into the kitchen. Neither of them looked "Russian." I started to say something, but the one with the gun shushed me.

The other came back and helped me off with my coat, then handcuffed me and gagged me with a piece of black cloth. I made urgent gestures in the direction of the bathroom; he escorted me there and took off the cuffs; left the door open but stood politely with his back to me. There was nothing obvious in the bathroom clutter that I could use as a weapon. A twin-blade Lady Gillette wouldn't do much against a machine gun anyhow.

So these were some of Nick's KGB buddies. I guessed they had found out about the CIA guy and wanted to put some pressure on Nick. But this wasn't at all like the mundane spy stuff he had told me about. I was suddenly in the middle of a movie.

They sat me down at the dining room table and went back into the kitchen to whisper at each other in Russian, or some other Slavic language. The armed one returned after a few minutes and handed me a notepad with a message something like this: "You and I are going someplace else. Pick up whatever you need for a few days. We have a car downstairs. If you try to escape or cry out on the way I will kill you."

I got my toothbrush and a paper bag of clothes and such. Several paperback books and a handful of mail that was sitting on the dining room table. My escort put his gun in an attaché case and went through the pockets of my coat. He found the Mace squirter, wiped his fingerprints off it, and tossed it under the couch. Then he handed me the coat, dropped the handcuffs into his pocket, and motioned for us to go.

A part of my brain that I couldn't make shut up was saying, This is deep shit. These guys are kidnapping you and they aren't even bothering to wear masks. Either they are rank amateurs or they know that you'll never live to identify them.

There was a dark-green van waiting in front of the apartment building. Getting in, I contrived to drop a piece of mail on the sidewalk, but he saw me do it. Retrieved it and handed it back without comment.

In the back of the van there were no windows, just

a lumpy carpet and a pair of incongruous easy chairs, overstuffed and musty, and a picnic cooler. I sat down, and he handcuffed me to the cooler, then rummaged around in it and offered me a Coke. I said no, but he opened it and pressed it into my free hand. Then he shook a pill out of a bottle and held it out for me to take. I didn't make an issue of it. It was a little yellow pill like aspirin for children, but very bitter.

The van drove off down Harvard Street, away from the river and Boston. After a few blocks my vision started to blur and I felt a little sick. I drank some more of the Coke and then dropped the can, on the verge of vomiting, but then I went totally limp and couldn't keep my head up or my eyes open. With my head vibrating against the cold window my last thought was *Twenty years ago I would have paid good money for this shit.*

CHAPTER NINE

JACOB

THE FEELING IS like *déjà vu* inside out: You should know something, remember something, but you don't. There's just a hole there. Whatever kind of magicking Foley pulled on me, it worked absolutely. They show me his picture, and it means nothing to me. Yet I spent dozens of hours talking to the man, hundreds of hours studying him, and even went to Europe with him.

Europe is the horror. Not his erasing my memory —no, he was gentle with me. It was the videotape we got from the French police, through the *Sûreté:* the Bulgarian secret agent who, after shooting his companion four times in the heart, had shot himself in the head; his skull on the left shattered and dribbling brains, his eyeball extruded and lolling on his cheek —but still he was miraculously alive. In a rambling mélange of French, Russian, Turkish, and Bulgarian he told how Foley had ordered him and the other agent to go on a long train ride, as far as their money would take them, and then walk out of town to where they would not be seen, and die. For seven hours they knew they were riding to self-inflicted death, and they could do nothing to prevent it. Perhaps not "nothing." A bullet to the brain evidently broke the spell.

The agent died during the filming, while the doctors were working on him. Langley has sent out a team of forensic specialists to assist in the autopsy. Maybe they'll find a drug.

What Foley did to me was comic by comparison. I woke up in Orsay, a suburb of Paris, in bed with a strange woman, with a red-wine hangover beyond epic proportions. I had been drinking—guzzling, actually—for three days, singlehandedly killing a case of a Burgundy that I find here in Boston runs eighty dollars a bottle. The woman said we had met in a Left Bank bistro, and one thing had led to another. She was worried about me, barely able to stand up but flashing a fat roll of francs, and brought me home with her; I evidently drank compulsively from dawn till dark until the three days were up. She said it was a hilarious time. I wish I could remember something of what went on. I don't suppose Foley was entirely responsible for that particular amnesia.

By this time the grotesque videotape had made its way to Washington, and the proper connections had been made, and the police all over France were on the lookout for my body. (My passport had wound up in a mailbox at Dulles International, with Foley's fingerprints all over it.) When I staggered into the *gendarmerie* in Orsay, the police quite properly acted as if they'd seen a ghost, and unfortunately repaid my benefactress by throwing her in le slammer for several hours, over my protests. I had written down her address, though, and mailed her all my leftover francs, about five hundred dollars' worth—God knows where and how Foley got them; my own traveler's checks were untouched.

The *Sûreté* had also sent copies of the tape to the

Bulgarian and Soviet authorities. The Russians made an initial loud noise and then said nothing. "Someone"—the French did not give their sources—had seen Foley leave the hotel with the two Bulgarians and then return an hour or so later, alone. Then he spent some time with me in the hotel bar, where he was seen to slip me some cash. Then he walked out of the hotel, into the Metro, and was never seen again.

From this side, all we know is that he landed in Dulles November 16, having booked first-class passage on the Concorde in my name. Paid cash. He set off the metal detector but convinced the guard that he had a pacemaker, which is not true. A *Peace*maker is more likely; we know he's an expert pistol shot and has at least two unregistered weapons. From Dulles he might have taken the subway straight to National and stepped on the shuttle to Boston—no ID required with cash, of course—or to anyplace on the East Coast. Or he could have rented a car and driven to Akron or Tulsa. We know he did call home, but not necessarily from a local phone.

That's where it gets complicated in an especially ugly way. When the videotape finally found its way to Washington and the computer identified Foley as being my section's responsibility, somebody ran back the tapes of the phone tap and their apartment bugs. Silence for the past day and a half. The afternoon of the sixteenth, though, we could hear the apartment being broken into. The "burglars" said nothing; just waited in place until Mrs. Foley came home. There was a brief struggle; they evidently tied her up and gagged her. That night, Foley called, and one of them answered the phone with "We have your wife," in Russian. Foley hung up and has not called since. The two agents evidently kidnapped Mrs. Foley.

Which is remarkable. The KGB rarely indulges in serious crime outside of Communist countries. They must be as scared as we are over Foley. But more efficient: From the time the videotape was turned over to the Soviet embassy in Paris to the apartment break-in, slightly more than four hours elapsed.

My obvious first move was to pay a visit to Vladimir Borachev, Foley's ultimate superior here, and ask whether he had committed any capital crimes lately. I was on my way out the door when I literally ran into David Jefferson.

He was a formidable-looking man, a black Charles Atlas. Handsome features modified by a webbed scar that ran from cheekbone to ear. He asked if I was John Jacob Bailey and handed me an envelope.

The letter inside informed me that Jefferson had been "attached" to my section for an indefinite period. The verb was to become too literally true.

"You're a Marine sergeant major?"

"That is correct, sir." He had a voice like a bass buzz saw.

"And this one hundred ninety-ninth Brigade is . . ."

"Special antiterrorism unit, sir."

"Please don't call me 'sir.' We aren't being hijacked or held hostage. Why were you attached to us?"

"The kidnapping, Mr. Bailey. The murders in France."

"You've been well briefed, then."

"Not that well, actually. The fact of the crimes; the KGB connection."

"Well, have George get you the folder, George Simpson. When he gets back from lunch. I have a shuttle to catch."

"I'm coming with you."

"Not necessary. In fact, you'd be in the way. Unless you speak Russian."

"—I'm reasonably fluent," he said in Russian, with an odd accent that might have been Vietnamese. "Also Spanish and a bit of a few other languages. But that's immaterial at the moment. I'm to accompany you everywhere, regardless."

"Bodyguard?"

"Yes, but more than that. A plain bodyguard wouldn't be enough. What they say about this Foley, he might be the most dangerous man alive, and you're his most logical next victim."

"Nonsense. If he wanted to do me in, he could have done it in Paris."

"That may be so. Nevertheless, I have my orders. As have you." The letter was from Langley.

"Oh, all right. Let's go." I barely had time to worry about how to handle the red tape—how to bill the Marines for his shuttle flight—when Jefferson solved the problem by suggesting that we "manifest ourselves on a special flight," i.e., commandeer a military aircraft. I could see that he might sometimes be handy to have around.

Sitting by ourselves in the back of a twenty-passenger turboprop, we got to know each other a little. Jefferson was a few years younger than I; started at West Point but dropped out to join the Marines, so he could make it to Vietnam before the war was over. He served fourteen months' duty there and was not happy when we pulled out. Later he was an "adviser" in El Salvador and, temporarily out of the Marines, did some wet work in Nicaragua. Wounded eleven times; the scar on his face was from a bayonet (he had taken the weapon away and "fed it" to its owner). He was obviously on amiable terms with mayhem, but was matter-of-fact about it. Unnervingly so.

When he unbuttoned his Harris Tweed tent of a jacket, you could see he was actually a fraction smaller than he appeared, bulked out on the right by an Ingram machine pistol Velcro-ed to his side, and on the left by a cross-draw .44 Magnum. He was also wearing body armor and advised me to requisition same. Said it had saved his life twice. I suspected that bullets would bounce off him anyhow.

I told him in a blunt but, I hope, friendly way that I considered him a liability. An agent has to fade into the background, look like a bank clerk or a school-marm. He can't have a Sherman tank for a pet.

Surprisingly, he agreed. But he pointed out that this was no normal intelligence operation; everyone involved would know that I was CIA anyhow. His presence might make people think twice before trying anything dramatic.

We got to the Soviet trade mission by two o'clock. The outer office was large and severe, a few faded Intourist posters not livening things up. The receptionist also was large and severe. She told us that Comrade Borachev saw people by appointment only. I showed her my State Department identification. She said Comrade Borachev wasn't in today. Maybe on vacation.

It was a good thing we'd seen a file photo of him; he walked in at just that moment, brushing snow off his shoulders and looking expectantly friendly.

"Mr. Borachev," I began.

"—He's from the State Department," she snapped in Russian.

"—Actually, the CIA," I said. "—This is a matter of great urgency. No time for games."

"We can speak English," he said slowly. He looked at Jefferson. "You are also from . . ."

"U.S. Marines, sir. Security."

"You don't expect violence."

"We don't know what to expect," I said. "Is there someplace we could talk?"

"My office." He walked toward the door, and we followed. He cut off Jefferson. "Actual spies only, please." I nodded, feeling a little apprehensive, and Jefferson reluctantly eased onto a small chair.

Borachev's office was comfortably cluttered. He got us each a cup of coffee and sat down behind his desk. The only other chair was a few inches lower. He smiled down at me, a wan smile. "So you have some interest in the import-export business?"

"As I say, there's not time to be coy. I'm sorry to hand you such a shock. I'm sure that the Agency would much rather leave you alone in place—"

"'Better the devil you know,'" he said.

"Right. But many lives may be at stake. We have to move quickly."

"Forgive me for pointing out that this is a common American trait, certainly in business: perceiving a need for haste in all things." He looked quizzical. "Many lives?"

"Yes. What do you know of Nicholas Foley? Do you know where he is?"

For a long time he chewed at his lower lip. "I think I had better not answer that. If you press me, I'll have to get a lawyer."

"Let me spell it out for you. I know and you know that you are a rather high-ranking officer, a colonel in the KGB. But your official identity here carries no legal perquisites. No diplomatic immunity. And you are implicated in a kidnapping and at least two murders." His brow furrowed at that, but he didn't say anything. "Gas chamber," I added helpfully.

He covered his face with both hands and kneaded.

"No. This is some kind of . . . CIA trick. Setting me up, as you would say."

"Nothing of the kind. Day before yesterday, two people kidnapped Valerie Foley. They spoke Russian."

"Valerie Foley, that is his wife?"

"Yes."

He nodded, thoughtful. "It wasn't anybody from the KGB. You had better look to your own house. I'm sure the CIA has many Russian-speaking employees."

"The CIA didn't kidnap her. If we wanted to pressure Foley, we have dozens of legal ways to do it. You don't."

"But neither do we have a *reason*!"

I had to laugh at that. "Two murdered KGB agents isn't enough reason?"

He leaned back, chair squeaking. "All right. Now I know something, uh, fishy is going on. Some sort of game."

"Not a game."

"I've known Professor Foley since he was a young man. Since we were both young men. He's not capable of violence."

"A few days ago, I would have agreed with you. He's a gentle, pleasant man. But either that's a mask or he is genuinely mad. Perhaps in the sense of having more than one personality. Look at this." I handed him two grisly still photographs we had made from the *Sûreté* tape. "I do think he's mad."

"My word." Borachev looked genuinely repulsed. "You claim Nicola did this?"

"Worse—he compelled them to do it to themselves. The one who shot himself in the head lived long enough to tell. He has some sort of Svengali-like power. We don't know what the limits of it could be.

I know it sounds fantastic, but it's true. That Marine says they're calling him the most dangerous man alive. Probably no exaggeration."

"All right. I do know where he is." He opened a desk drawer and fished around inside. "I have the hotel name in here somewhere; he's in Paris."

I laughed. "Not anymore. Not since he killed those two."

"Ah." He looked at the pictures again. "These are the KGB agents?"

"Bulgarian KGB."

He pursed his lips, nodding, and handed back the pictures. "That could be why I don't know more about this than I do."

"You think the Bulgarian KGB might be behind the kidnapping?"

"Oh, possibly. That's not what I mean, though. You know." He flapped a hand, thinking. "It's true that I'm an officer in the Soviet army, as you say, in the KGB division. But my daily connection with the KGB is as tenuous as yours would be with the American army if, say, you were a colonel in the Reserves. I'm not a *spy*. I'm an import-export analyst and adviser, who keeps his eyes open. You see the distinction I'm making?"

"What you mean is that the KGB could be behind it without your having been notified. Even the Soviet KGB."

He shrugged. "If you were this Reserve colonel in the American Army, would the army ask your advice before invading some small island? Would the Navy? I think not." There was a knock on the door. "Come in."

The receptionist walked in with a frozen scowl. Behind her was Jefferson, the .44 dangling.

"Jefferson," I said with some pain in my voice,

"this is not Vietnam. You're not supposed to point guns at people and march them around."

"It was a judgment call." He gestured with the weapon, and all three of us flinched in unison. "I think you're fishin' in the wrong hole. She assumed that a big black dumb Marine couldn't speak Russian. Made a phone call. I felt I had to interrupt it."

"Who was the call to?"

"Don't know. Called him *tarakan*, 'cockroach.' I don't guess that's a name in Russia. Maybe a term of endearment."

"Yeah, code. Who was it?" I asked her.

She ignored me. "You have broken the laws of the state of New York. You are a dangerous hooligan, and I will take you to court."

He laughed. "Yeah, you'll see me in court, all right."

Borachev was looking at her as if he'd never seen her before. "—Please, Galina. We have enough trouble." She answered with one syllable of dismissal.

"What was she talking about?"

Jefferson showed many square teeth too perfect to be real. "She told the cockroach that Borachev was about to betray them. She tried to listen in, and the gizmo didn't work."

Borachev reached into the open drawer and pulled out a small button microphone. "This is yours, Galina? I was just going to tell you about it; I thought it was—"

"You stay quiet. For your own good if not for... principles."

"What do you know about Nicholas Foley?" I asked her. "About the kidnapping of Foley's wife?"

"I know nothing about anything." She didn't look at me, still glaring at Borachev.

"You're withholding evidence pertaining to capital crimes."

"I know all about *crimes* in this country. You can't make me talk."

"She's only been with the firm for two weeks," Borachev said with no irony. "She has some odd ideas about America."

"You have some odd ideas, Comrade Borachev."

"Which is why you were sent to replace me?" She made a disgusted noise and stalked over to stare down at the East River, her back to us. Borachev turned to me. "No matter what she thinks . . . I am not going to be on your side. I will be of whatever aid I can be in the criminal aspects of this, this murder. But you cannot expect me to betray my country. Not even to stay out of prison."

"—Such a patriot," she said venomously.

"—Such a *pain!*"

"Jefferson," I said, "do you have an FBI contact number?" He did. "Have them come collect her. Our liaison on the Foley case is Herb Stratton in Washington; have them check in with him." He escorted her to the outer office and we sat back down.

"What I said was true. You can't turn me. I will allow you to convince me that this is serious enough for me to give you limited cooperation."

"Good," I said. "I can't promise anything, but it could be the difference between jail and deportation." I seemed to be offering that choice to a lot of people lately.

"Wonderful. If I could only decide which would be better."

CHAPTER TEN

NICK

FASTING FOR TWO weeks, with cautious exercise, I managed to reduce my beer belly to reasonable proportions. Working up to an hour a day on the sunlamp, I started to look less like a bookworm and more like a farmer or sportsman.

I stayed in the Bangor-Portland area, changing motels every two days. Both cities had university libraries; I spent a lot of time in each. A little research. A lot of thinking. Or at least a lot of worrying.

When I was young and philosophical, I thought that I would be able to live a blameless life governed by Kant's Categorical Imperative: *Act as if the maxim of thy action were to become by thy will a universal law of nature, on which every other person would act.* The agnostic's all-purpose do-unto-others; the eightfold path boiled down to one hard step.

It does work well for moral and ethical problems of a universal nature: Should I take a chance on getting the girl in trouble? Should I go off to war, help my friend cheat on the exam, tell the boss that Bob's a slacker, bring children into a world of pain? Hard questions, but everybody has to answer them.

It's not so easy to apply the Imperative to a singularity: a problem that no other person has ever experienced and probably never will. You are the Soviet premier and president; you have authorized missiles to be sent to an ally nation being bullied by a mutual enemy. The enemy orders a blockade and implies that there will be war if the missile bases aren't dismantled. Nuclear war. But he's probably bluffing. What do you do? How could you reasonably apply the Imperative? No other person in the world is in a position to decide; it's meaningless to claim that your decision would be "right" for someone else. It has to be right, period. You have to admit that you are special and that for you there are no rules, only results.

So that is the large problem, the "meta-problem," which I have been putting off for such a long time, using this power essentially at the party-trick level. The party trick of serial murder.

I could become the most powerful person in the world. Perhaps in the history of the world. All I would have to do would be to talk myself into proximity with one world leader after another and tell them what I want done. Only China would be beyond my grasp—and then only so long as she keeps a premier who speaks no foreign language. Or until I learn Chinese.

But I have no agenda to save humanity, no righteous or even selfish itch for that kind of power. All I desire is quite the reverse: immunity *from* power, from the powerful. An orderly, bookish sort of existence, occasionally spiced. As I have had for most of my life. Now, I suppose, that's no longer possible.

Perhaps the course most morally defensible would be suicide. I should destroy the watch and then myself. Any government that learns that watch's simple secret could, with radio and television broadcasts, make its citizens do anything. Not only its citizens;

anyone who comes within earshot. (Would there be an underground of deaf persons? Of people intentionally made deaf in the higher frequencies?) But suicide is unthinkable to me and has been since I was old enough to understand that some people do it, that many of my neighbors had done it—which was perhaps too young. It could be that extreme adversity divides us into two groups: those who are able to surrender to the shadow of death and those who will hang on to life even when it promises nothing but a few more days or minutes of pain. Perhaps the will to survive and survive regardless, once discovered, becomes a reflex attitude that permeates the rest of your life.

At any rate, having rejected the most sensible and simple course, I am now embarked on a rather Byzantine one. In both the *Boston Globe* and the *New York Times,* this message has appeared in the personals: "NF—VF wants to talk to you," followed by Boston and New York phone numbers. And so of course I'm going to Washington.

But not right away. I have to assume that Valerie will be safe so long as they're still looking for me, and my best chance for rescuing her will be to bide my time until I know enough about the situation to sneak up, free her, and disappear before anyone really knows what's happening. And do it all without leaving tracks.

My first impulse was to go back to Boston and use the watch on a phone-company person and find out what address corresponds to the number in the paper. Then go rescue her, nonviolently if possible.

A few times each waking hour, and sometimes while asleep, I wish that I had done just that. My nature is to move cautiously, and having charge of this machine makes me triply cautious. But in my own heart I will never be free from the charge of cowardice. If my caution has cost her life, I will die.

But the ones who put that ad in the papers won't simply be sitting in a room, waiting for the phone to ring. Not with my known association with the CIA, and those two dead Bulgarians, assuming they were found. I must assume that they have been. There will certainly be guards outside, and electronic surveillance. "Action at a distance" is the key.

This should have happened ten years ago; it would have been easier to change my appearance then. The scale says I've lost eleven pounds, and indeed I look fairly trim if I keep my abdomen sucked in like a drill sergeant. If I relax, my chest falls half a meter.

I bought a second belt and wear it under my shirt at navel level when I go out, to serve as a reminder. It's tiring but seems to work. It will probably have a salutary effect on my digestion, when I start eating regularly again.

With the help of the phenylalanine I could have starved for another couple of weeks and will do so now that I've found another hiding place. But running took energy, and I did have to run. Jacob, or somebody, forced my hand. They might have caught me with subtlety. Instead they tried force.

I woke up at dawn to a strange traffic sound. Looked out the window and was surprised to see an army convoy.

Television news said that it was "maneuvers"— they just happened to order half of New England's National Guard into a perimeter around Bangor . . . while, "in an unrelated story," the FBI was searching Bangor for a murderer on the fifteen-most-wanted list. Have you seen this man? The picture looked like a portly gentleman with glasses and a Santa Claus beard. Not at all like me.

I remembered reading, though, that nobody gets on that list unless the FBI is pretty confident that they'll be captured soon. So I moved, as they used to say, with a purpose.

I gathered up my few things and drove across town to a motel where I hadn't stayed before. Loitered for a while and then borrowed a car from a new patron right after he checked in, suggesting that he sleep for at least twelve hours. I got past the roadblock by telling the private I was his company commander. (He was taking a picture of each person, but I asked that he skip me.) I drove toward the coast and stopped at the first small airfield; took a puddle jumper to Boston and shuttled Logan–LaGuardia–National. Caught the next Eastern flight to Atlanta, then Miami, and by sundown I was just another tourist strolling along the docks at Key West. Salty fresh-fish cucumber smell and flowers I couldn't identify. Compared to the austere Maine winter, a riot of sensation. Jugglers shouting and laughing, singing buskers with their hats out, a contortionist, people hawking carnival food and tropical drinks. A girl on a bicycle with a Styrofoam box, selling chocolate-chip cookies still warm from the oven. I had broken my fast slightly with bites from two damp airline sandwiches, which had made me feel vaguely ill. One cookie awakened the hungry beast in me. I ate four more before I got control of myself.

Valerie and I had visited Key West for a conference in the late seventies but hadn't seen any of the other Keys, being carless and fairly broke. We'd been especially intrigued by a place called No Name Key, about thirty miles away. I asked around and found out there was nothing there but a fishing camp. That sounded good, and the name was certainly right for a person in my situation. I bought a rod and reel and some appropriate clothing, filled a cooler with various fruit juices, and drove out there in a Rent-A-Wreck.

You couldn't see anything at night, and I was dead-tired anyhow from running all day. But at dawn I knew I'd made the right choice. December sun burning away early mist, stillness only broken by jumping fish and the occasional cries of odd wading birds. Even a small alligator. A good place to drop another ten pounds, work on my tan, read a dozen books.

Rest up for the assault.

CHAPTER ELEVEN

JACOB

HE MADE A mistake, fingerprints. But then we made a bigger one.

Actually, he left just one fingerprint. That was enough, with the FBI's computers and organizational power. Plus a good portion of luck, which unfortunately didn't last.

First this young man showed up at Logan, fresh off a plane from Las Vegas, with a fat roll of used twenties and no memory of the past nine days. He reported a stolen car, a van, and since the interviewing officer's report mentioned the key word *amnesia*, the FBI computer's "expert system" flagged it.

The van's engine surfaced in a parts store in Albany. With some impromptu plea bargaining and perhaps muscle, the FBI tracked down the boy who had stolen it. He led them to the van's body, which had been repainted and was doing service delivering sheetrock. Most of the interior had been stripped, but they went over every square inch of it anyhow. With an infrared laser they found a full set of prints from an Albany woman who had also recently suffered amnesia, evidently right after her high school reunion in Bangor, Maine. On her purse they brought out one latent print from Nicholas Foley.

Jefferson and I found out about this some twelve hours after the FBI had set its wheels in motion. Weather had closed the Bangor airport; we got the first flight to Portland and drove the hundred-plus miles too fast for the conditions, to be caught in the largest traffic jam in Bangor's history. Hundreds of military vehicles had thrown a cordon around the town. It looked like the Normandy invasion with snow.

They had every road going out of Bangor blocked. They weren't stopping cars going into town, but they might as well have been, since everyone slowed down to gawk. Jefferson turned our rented Dodge Dart into an off-the-road vehicle, and we passed everybody on the far right, chains digging up the real estate. A jeep full of MPs came after us and attempted to cut us off, television style, which doesn't work in a vacant lot. Jefferson steered a four-wheel drift around them, laughing. They cut us off again and then pulled guns. Jefferson slammed on the brakes, jumped out, and stalked toward them holding his identification out in front of him, like a priest warding off vampires with a crucifix, though with unpriestly language. The MPs were in the right, just following orders, but he had more rank than all of them put together, as well as histrionic ability and decibels. Black Conan on angel dust.

So we had a chastized escort to the lieutenant colonel who was in charge of the operation. Jefferson was all deference with him, and he in turn deferred to the mystery of my three Agency initials. With his help, we pieced together most of the story.

About half of these people had been out on a winter field exercise. At the request of the FBI, they

mobilized the other two battalions, and they all con-
verged on Bangor. All the officer knew was that there
was a dangerous murderer inside the city limits, trying to get out. He was full of questions about the CIA
involvement. I told him to keep it secret, and he assured me he would, but there was a gleam in his eye.
I was going to be the bombshell he would drop at the
officers' mess tonight after dinner.

We found my opposite number from the FBI, Don-
ald Chang, at an improvised communications center
in the sheriff's dispatcher's office. He was mortified
about all the soldiers; it hadn't been his idea. (We
never did find out who was responsible for the excess.) He had asked for as much help as he could get
from the state and local police, especially of the
SWAT variety, but somewhere along the line his concern had been greatly amplified.

The FBI and police had already checked every
motel and rooming house, with the predictable result
that nobody could remember anyone who looked like
him ever checking in. Hell, I'd been to Europe with
him, and I couldn't remember what he looked like!

We emptied all of the bank cameras, and again the
FBI's expert systems came to our aid. They pushed
about a million pictures through an optical scanning
device, and it returned forty-some pictures of people
who looked like Foley. One was him. We checked the
bank and found that he had cashed two thousand dollars' worth of traveler's checks, made out to Porfiry
Petrovitch. That was the name of the detective in
Crime and Punishment. Funny.

But a few pieces were falling into place. The
teller's machine noted that all of the two thousand had
been paid out in twenties. The boy who'd lost the van
and gained a roll of twenties had complained that he
felt "terminally tired." No wonder; we found that

he'd turned in a subcompact rental car in Los Angeles two days before he showed up in Boston. So he'd driven coast-to-coast in seven days of snowy weather, bent double in a sardine can.

I'd been more than half afraid that we'd find a trail of bodies leading to Foley—or leading to the last place he'd been. That he'd gone to this kind of trouble with the boy was a good sign. He could have just told him to drive into a wall. Possibly those two Bulgarian agents had done something to deserve their fate.

We did have a timetable. Foley got to Bangor the day after he came back from Paris. That afternoon he went to the bank. The next morning he rented the boy's subcompact; within the next twenty-four hours he compelled the Albany woman to drive the van away and abandon it in New York. After that, he either stayed in Bangor or went someplace else. Maybe Portland. Maybe Portland, Oregon. Maybe Singapore.

The FBI was diligently dusting and laser-beaming every motel and hotel room in Bangor. That's a lot of rooms. Foley was evidently careful about fingerprints. I wasn't sure it was worth the effort. They would come up with a print and the clerk would remember having rented the room to a six-foot-five Chinaman with an eyepatch and a parrot.

CHAPTER TWELVE

NICK

I DIDN'T CATCH as many fish as the other patrons staying at No Name Key, since I rarely used bait. I did row out every morning, not toward the Gulf, where the serious fishing was, but inland. There were quiet bayous where I could drift, reading, uninterrupted for hours. Baking in the sun and listening to my stomach growl.

How long to wait? I didn't have to starve myself to rail thinness. I did want to hold off my next move long enough for the initial enthusiasm of the CIA and KGB—and the FBI and whoever else was involved —to wear off; long enough for their energies to diffuse. Christmas passed by, and New Year's. I started eating again and stabilized my weight at 160. The figure in the mirror looked gaunt to me, especially the face, which probably meant it looked about average to other people. That was what I wanted, of course. Clean-shaven with a fringe of white hair, I had little in common with my former appearance other than height. Any picture they might dig up of me without a beard would be more than a quarter century old. No doubt they did have computer programs and artists who could calculate or guess what I look like now, if they made the right assumptions. *What would Nicholas Foley look like if he dropped forty pounds and got a tan,* et cetera? I wasn't worried.

After erasing the memory of my stay from the minds of the fishing-camp landlord and the people who ran the 7-Eleven and the No Name Bar and Grill, I returned the car to Key West and took a bus up to Miami. Bought a complete wardrobe of quietly expensive businessman uniforms, some new, some used; some well-worn "favorites" that were almost shabby. Night flight to Washington, and by noon the next day I was comfortably established in a Georgetown efficiency.

I spent all of that day making up a tentative past for the person I was going to be. Solid academic career in languages, steady industrial consultant work; service in Korea—gave myself a Purple Heart and slight disability, for federal employment preference —a Peace Corps posting in the sixties, extensive but ideologically safe foreign travel. Publications in conservative and neoconservative journals as well as the more technical linguistic outlets. Thinking of retiring from my academic position if something more interesting presents itself. Like the CIA.

To document the career, at least after a fashion, I had to find a real person of approximately the right age and background, so that "I" would exist in reference books. Nobody with a career of any distinction can stay out of *Who's Who*—type texts, at least the specialized ones. So I riffled through the Modern Language Association source book looking for somebody who was close to my manufactured profile.

James Norwood filled the bill. Two years older than I was, brought up in the East but now tenured at the University of Nebraska, having been there since the early seventies. So I could wander the halls of the

CIA with little risk of running into Norwood's current lover. Or Norwood himself, though that was easily taken care of.

It would be nice if the signal generator worked over the phone. Save me a trip to Lincoln, Nebraska, which is no garden spot in the dead of winter.

I flew out on the red-eye to Chicago and met Norwood in his office the next morning. It turned out— bless tenure!—that he taught only one class, a weekly seminar, which was easily cancelled.

He was to tell people that he was going to Washington for a couple of weeks of "consultation"—but confide in his wife and one close friend that it involved a hush-hush job interview. Then go someplace *not* Washington and come back with a made-up story about not landing the job.

He generously gave me copies of the two books he'd written on Russian dialects, which I read during the interminable wait at O'Hare, and on the flight back. He writes well in Russian but has a tin ear for English.

Of course I couldn't expect my substitution to stand up to the rigorous security clearance a normal person would have to undergo before getting a job with the CIA. I was assuming that I could subvert someone fairly low in the chain of command and have my application taken out of the normal sequence of checks. Have to be most careful; assume hidden microphones everywhere. And cover my tracks when I leave. Jim Norwood? Oh, yeah, he went back to Lincoln a couple of weeks ago. Thought I had his address here somewhere . . .

I didn't plan on staying long. Just long enough to find out whether it was they or the KGB who had kidnapped Valerie, and perhaps find out where she was being held. Then get on my white horse and charge. Or perhaps sneak up and slip knockout gas into the air conditioning. Maybe someone in the CIA could tell me where to get the stuff.

It was after midnight by the time I had everything completely mapped out. Couldn't sleep. I went down by Seventh Street and watched a mugger in an alley slit his own throat.

Then I could sleep, no dreams.

CHAPTER THIRTEEN

VALERIE

THEY HELD ME for eighty-nine days before anyone said anything to me, though my guards did understand English. The first pair spoke Russian to each other; the second, a man and a woman, never talked at all.

I was moved three times, drugged. The second move took all day, and I vaguely remember having been rolled into an airplane, so now I could be anywhere in the country. I never see a newspaper, of course, and there's no clue from the food, which either comes out of a can or was excreted through the Golden Arches. (I went on a hunger strike for a couple of days, demanding real food, but they just watched me, setting out a fresh hamburger every few hours.) I had fantasies about bean curd and alfalfa sprouts.

Six weeks in this long, dark room, most of the time handcuffed to a chair. I should have done isometric exercises from the start; now it's too late. I couldn't make it to the bathroom without an arm to lean on.

One morning, the eighty-ninth, the woman cleaned up the cans from breakfast and left me alone for a minute. That was a curious sensation, being unattended, since I hadn't even been allowed to bathe without an audience.

It was a strange room, with the proportions of a bowling-alley lane, long and narrow. Black walls with light only at my end, except when the door at the other end was opened and dim light came in from the corridor. That happened, and a new man came in.

He was short and chubby and dressed in a dark, cheap suit that was a size too small. A narrow tie many seasons out of date was cinched up so tight that the fat of his neck rolled over his collar. He looked like a small-town postmaster or some such minor self-important bureaucrat, but he was conspicuously armed, a heavy pistol dragging down his right coat pocket.

There was one other chair at the small dining room table. He moved it three inches, so that it was directly across from me, brushed off the seat with a handkerchief, and carefully sat down. He planted both elbows on the table and folded his hands under his chin. "I want you to answer some questions," he said with a Boston "awn-seh." I just looked at him.

"We're having trouble locating your husband."

"Is that so?" My voice sounded strange to me.

"He knows what number to call. Two numbers. Presumably he knows that not calling places you in danger."

That was something I'd had some time to think about. "Maybe not. Maybe he assumes that if he calls, you'll make some threat concerning me, and he'll have to—"

"I would be careful with these 'maybes,'" the man said testily, mocking. "*May*be he assumes that you're dead. In which case you are simply a drain on our resources, and a risk."

"Whose resources?"

"Don't worry about that yet."

"I won't tell you a thing unless I know who I'm talking to."

He smiled; small, pursed lips. "All right. If I say CIA, will you believe me? Or KGB? Would you like to see my Mafia identification card?"

"Very funny." I leaned forward. "But yes. My husband said he met a CIA man, who had a State Department ID card. Let's see yours."

"Come now. Anyone can have a card printed up."

"That's right. But *you* didn't."

He looked at me for a long moment. "I don't suppose it makes any difference. Yes, like your husband, I am a KGB agent."

"Okay. Then answer the obvious question. Why are you—"

"I may answer some questions if I'm satisfied with your own answers."

"No, you first."

"I have the gun." Suddenly there was a small pistol in his left hand. *Literally* suddenly; no blur of motion, no noise. Just a sudden gun, and not the one still bulging his pocket.

"How did you do that?"

"Trick of the trade." He rubbed his hands together and it was gone. "Your husband's trade, I remind you."

"My husband was never involved in anything to do with guns. And you can't make me—"

He rose halfway out of his chair and slapped me on the lips, lightly, but with that snakelike speed. Then he held his hand out in front of me. There was a single-edged razor palmed between thumb and finger.

"Think," he said. "Pretty lips." Then he slipped out of the chair and was too quickly standing by the door. "Next time we will discuss your husband . . . and his guns."

I felt the violating touch, almost a caress, for some time afterward.

CHAPTER FOURTEEN

NICK

HOW DO YOU get a job as a spy? The location of the Langley, Virginia, headquarters of the CIA isn't kept secret nowadays, but you would feel conspicuous driving to the end of the long, deserted road and asking the heavily armed guards for a job application. People probably do it. I thought I'd have better luck downtown on C Street, at the State Department Office of Intelligence and Research, Personnel Section.

I took a senior clerk to lunch after convincing her I was a long-lost college chum. She wanted to eat in the cafeteria downstairs, but I insisted on something fancier. The State Department might or might not snoop on its employees while they were on home turf, but I was pretty sure they wouldn't have any microphones hidden in a popular seafood restaurant a ten-dollar cab ride away.

It was a long lunch and a productive one. She memorized the various data to be entered into the personnel system and explained how she could get around the hidden redundancy checks.

She had been at the State Department for more than twenty-five years. I "suggested" that she start the paperwork for retirement. Her job wouldn't be worth a handful of shredded memos once they traced my path back to her, as they inevitably would. The wheels of the gods grind slow, but they grind everybody.

Washington was all cold slush and grime, so I was just as happy to have to stay home by the phone. Bought a bunch of books about the CIA. The reading was as much diversion as preparation. There was no point in planning ahead too carefully, since my course of action would be determined by what they knew about Valerie. But the more I knew about the Agency, the better I would be able to improvise.

I was surprised to hear from Langley the very next morning. Indeed they did have an opening, a quite specific one, for someone with my background. Would I come talk with Richard Goldman at my earliest convenience?

The cab driver was happy at the long fare and impressed by the destination. I tried to be suitably offhand and mysterious.

I'd expected some sort of cloak-and-dagger business at the guards' post, but they just waved us through. I made a joke about Iranian terrorists, and the driver laughed but looked around furtively.

That truck-bombing epidemic a few years back may have had some effect on the way the plant was arranged. There were lots of widely spaced low white buildings with no numbers or other markings apparent; no one building seemed more important than any other. The main road ended in a circle, where a building was identified with a discreet INFORMATION/RECEPTION sign. I paid the cabbie and he drove off very slowly.

I walked through an airport-style metal detector and identified myself to an unsmiling receptionist. She handed me a visitor's badge and a three-by-five card with terse typed directions. "Don't get lost," she said. "If you get lost, come right back here." Sound advice.

Goldman's office was underground, as most of the plant evidently was. Energy efficient. I took an elevator to Level C and walked down four long corridors left-right-left-left to his room number. Goldman had his door open, waiting for me.

He was a stocky, unkempt man with cowlicks and an easy smile. The office was plain government-gray, unadorned except for a reproduction of the old World War One poster "Loose Lips Sink Ships," upon which was thumbtacked a picture of a person with loose lips indeed.

He sat me down with coffee, emptied a half-full ashtray, and lit a new cigarette off the butt of his old one. "Wonderful coincidence, your application and clearance coming in just now. If I can talk you into taking the job."

"There's something wrong with it?"

"Just not very glamorous. Do you think espionage is glamorous?"

"I understand that it usually isn't." Except for the odd Bulgarian assassin or two.

"Listen to this." There was an old-fashioned German tape recorder on his desk, obviously once the top of its line, but now a reel-to-reel dinosaur. He stabbed a button, and a man's voice, distorted and blurred by noise, began speaking a truly weird brand of Russian. He let it go for about twenty seconds and turned it off. "You see the problem."

"Two problems. The bad recording I can't help you with. The dialect, I can. It's north Azerbaijanian. A rural accent, farmer." I was glad I'd refreshed my memory with Norwood's books, though of course I'd heard plenty of Azerbaijanian Russian spoken the years I was in Rivertown.

"What's he talking about?"

"Let me hear it again." It was fairly clear the second time. "It's a long-distance phone call; he's almost shouting. He's talking to someone named Kahn or Con, maybe a nickname for Constantine. They seem to be friends. He says there's an error in the projection figures for wheat production in his, Con's, district as regards some five-year plan. The figure is too low, and he's asking Con whom he bribed. From the inflection, though, he's joking. Maybe that's why it's so loud; he wants the other people in the office to overhear. Some of that background noise might be laughter."

"That's marvelous. You're exactly what we need. Do you like doing this kind of work?"

"Yes, indeed." In fact, I did.

"Well, we've got plenty of it, especially from around the Caucasus there. They seem to be assigning people with heavy and obscure accents to do telephone work in some sensitive areas, just to screw us up. Screws up their own operations, too, but"—he laughed and threw up his hands—"they're Russians. What can you say?"

I looked at him through the steam of the coffee and said in Russian, "—I think you like them."

"—I *love* them!" he said with a happy, atrocious American accent. "—I'm glad they're our enemies!" A reasonable sentiment, rather Russian. I took the job.

Goldman gave me a small office with an old word processor and a briefcase full of three-inch tapes to translate. It was absorbing work, entertaining the way crossword puzzles are, and for several days that's all I did. Then I started to cultivate a social relationship with Goldman, who was a lonely man and grateful for friends.

It was a cold-blooded thing to do, but necessary. I didn't dare give him any orders while we were in the office. In a succession of restaurants and theater lobbies, though, I set him up.

He'd been with the CIA for a long time and knew people in all parts of the organization. Through his casual conversations with people, I soon found out the main thing I wanted to know, which was that Valerie was being held by the KGB in some unknown place. Apparently, no one in the Agency had noticed the ads in the *Times* or the *Globe*.

They knew more about my power than I thought they would. One of the damned Bulgarians lived long enough to tell a horror story. That was the main reason they still had people chasing after Valerie.

The trail was growing cold. Two agents from the Boston regional office, Jacob Bailey and someone else, were following leads, but it had been some time since they'd come up with anything. At least one person on the case was sure Valerie was long dead.

If she was, a lot of people would pay.

Obviously, I had to go to the Boston office. But first there were various things I had to do at Langley.

All those years of hacking with MIT's Athena system paid off. I talked someone out of an A-Class clearance number and cautiously wormed my way into the CIA's murky computer system. I got to the personnel file on me as Norwood and jazzed it completely, changing my age and appearance, background, assignments. I made up a new character named Anson Rafferty, and gave *him* my appearance and fingerprints instead, just in case I wanted to come back. Anson took a little bit of research. He did some good work for the Agency way back when and had glowing references from a number of higher-ups, all of whom happened to have since graduated to that Old Boy Network in the sky, or the ground.

Not surprisingly, the system had a link to the FBI's data banks. I made sure that both agencies had bogus fingerprint sets for both me and Valerie.

I was startled, walking down a corridor one day, to run into Vladimir Borachev. I followed him and made up a pretext for getting him into conversation. I had the watch ready, but he didn't recognize me. He also spoke English with almost no Russian accent, which I suspect would surprise a lot of his agents.

From Goldman's sources I found out that Borachev was here under protective custody, in the process of telling all in exchange for immunity from prosecution. Once he was wrung dry, the CIA would give him Canadian papers and a one-way ticket to Toronto.

Would they make me a similar offer? I was not tempted to ask.

CHAPTER FIFTEEN

JACOB

I HAVE NEVER liked Chicago at all, which is not an unusual prejudice for a Bostonian. Any city you can't walk across in a couple of hours is too big. Plus it's too loud and smells bad and feels dangerous and the weather is like an alien planet's. The people drive like maniacs. At least that's a touch of home.

Jefferson and I got to circle O'Hare for ninety minutes, bouncing above a blizzard, while the ground crew cleaned up what was left of a light plane that had come in sideways. Our own landing was too exciting for my taste. The plane slithering down the runway through driven snow so thick you couldn't see any buildings. All for a wild goose chase, it turned out.

The FBI had agreed to get in touch with us if its surveillance of routine bank transactions turned up anything that involved Foley. They were putting considerably more man-hours and computer time into the case than they normally would even for large bank crimes, I suppose because what Foley could do to a KGB agent he could presumably do to one from the FBI.

So if he couldn't resist cashing another "Porfiry

Petrovitch" check, bells would ring from Washington to Los Angeles, and he wouldn't get out the door of the bank. But he evidently had figured that out, and kept his sense of humor restrained.

We wound up sliding down that runway because the same expert system that had identified Foley in Maine flagged the picture of a Chicago bank customer. Like Foley, he had cashed a number of traveler's checks, so he seemed like a good prospect. There was a day's delay, of course, since the bank pictures go on a tape and the tape has to be fed through an "analog converter/modem interface" after the bank closes. Then someone in Washington has to look through all the day's flagged images and decide which ones are interesting enough to warrant action. Then he contacts the proper department, and they contact the regional office, and the regional office wakes up a couple of agents and sends them out to wake up some bank personnel.

At any rate, this man "Daniel Wintrobe" was an absolute ringer for Foley—white beard, paunch, rumpled but expensive clothes. The teller, suspicious about his appearance, had asked for a verifiable address, for which he gave the name of a cheap but not too seedy South Side hotel. By telephone they'd confirmed he was a guest, but when the agents showed up the next day, all they found was an irate manager. The guy had stayed for a week and then skipped out in the middle of the night.

The FBI called it "bank fraud and suspicion of homicide" and told the Chicago police to find Wintrobe and put him under surveillance. Whoever had final responsibility evidently decided it would be easiest to keep him under surveillance inside a holding cell, a drunk tank. They slightly tenderized him in the process of moving him there.

One look and I knew he wasn't Foley. He was a middle-aged Skid Row denizen who belonged in some institution other than jail. He had a vague, confused gentleness that might have been alcoholic burnout or the early onset of Alzheimer's disease; maybe both. Sometimes he said he had found the clothes and checks; sometimes he said they were a gift from his daughter.

Through American Express the police had earlier found the real Daniel Wintrobe, who lived in Oak Park. He cautiously admitted that the checks were probably his. He didn't know he had lost them. No, he wouldn't press charges over the misappropriation of two hundred dollars; just have the remaining checks sent back to him. At the office address, please.

The desk sergeant's opinion was that the man was a "suburban faggot who don't want his wife to find out" and that he was probably rolled by a chickenhawk. How this ineffectual old man wound up with the checks and clothes, he couldn't explain. I suggested that maybe he mugged the chickenhawk. The sergeant asked if that was a joke.

We knew O'Hare would still be a madhouse, with all the people piling up from delayed flights. We probably could have flashed ID's and muscled our way onto a late flight back to the East Coast, but Jefferson had a better idea. We split the cost of a bottle of decent Scotch and got an overnight room at the Airport Hilton. Unfortunately for the taxpayers, the only rooms left were suites.

While I was calling the office, telling the answering machine where we were, Jefferson took a wedge-shaped lock out of his overnight bag and jammed it under the door. He checked it with all his considerable strength, and it held. Then he let me escape long enough to fill up the ice bucket.

It had been a long day. I shucked jacket and tie and shoes with the speed of an undergraduate and poured us each a drink. It took Jefferson longer to get comfortable. He hung up his jacket. Unslung the Ingram, released its magazine, made sure there was no round in the chamber. Hung it on the door. Shrugged out of the shoulder-holster harness and hung it up. Unzipped the Kevlar vest and hung it up. Carried the .44 over to the bed and set it on the nightstand, protecting the room-service menu. Then he took a big swallow of Scotch and loosened his tie. Sitting ramrod-straight on the bed, he methodically rolled his sleeves up to midforearm. Then he tipped the glass in my direction. "Cheers." He took a sip and lay back against the headboard, not too stiffly.

With any other man, it might have been a time for the letting down of hair, recalling of jokes and stories. There was something about Jefferson's thousand-yard stare that made it difficult to loosen up with him.

He did get a little reflective, though. "I guess you know I've worked with the Company before," he said, picking up the .44 Magnum.

I called it the Agency, myself, but let that pass. "Well, you said you were hurt in Nicaragua. I assume you didn't go there with the Salvation Army."

"Actually, that was a bunch of civilians, Texans. I got a leave of absence and went with them as an adviser." He ejected the cartridges one at a time onto the bed beside him. "Caught hell when I got back, too. No, it was in Vietnam I worked for the CIA."

"Wet work?"

"Huh-uh. Prisoner escort. It wasn't in my dossier?"

"I didn't get a dossier as such. Just one page, telling what a wonderful guy you were."

He did smile. He was polishing each cartridge with a handkerchief and standing them up in a little row next to the telephone. An odd thing to do. "Maybe it was unofficial. Orders I got supposedly sent me to be aide-de-camp for some colonel, but I never got to meet him. All the guys I worked for were civilian spooks."

"Wonder why they didn't use Agency personnel. For prisoner security, I mean."

"Nobody ever said. Keep their hands clean, I guess. Told me they'd asked for someone with a lot of confirmed kills."

"You killed prisoners? Like throwing them out of helicopters?"

"No, I never did that. I wasn't in helicopters much. Mostly Air America DC-3's." He clicked the cylinder around, squinting at it. "I heard of it, of course; everybody heard of it. But nobody ever ordered me to do it."

"Would you have done it if they'd ordered you to?"

"Wouldn't you?"

I hesitated and tried to be honest. "I don't think I could. But then I've never killed anybody."

"Yeah, you don't know. Nobody knows till it happens." He slid the shells methodically back into the cylinder. "If it was a direct order, I'd do it. Wouldn't much like it, but I'd do it."

"What if you knew he was innocent?"

"Innocent." He sighted down the barrel at the TV set and tensed, about to deliver the ultimate Nielson rating. "Orders are orders. Besides, everybody's innocent. Enemy soldiers are just innocent jerks who were too dumb to stay out of the army. Like most of us."

"Yet you don't mind killing them?"

He set the revolver down and smiled again. "It's a living."

The phone rang, and I picked it up. It was Harriet Leusner, our de facto boss in the Foreign Resources Division, down at Langley. I got the scrambler out of my shaving kit and managed to get it working, then gave her a nonreport. She expressed no surprise and passed on a couple of tidbits of information.

I hung up and left the scrambler in place for the time being. "Any news?" Jefferson asked.

"That 'cockroach' the woman was talking to, they've come up with zilch. They have a tap and trace on the phone at the trade mission, of course, but the guy was talking from a pay phone in Port Authority."

"But she called him, not the other way around."

"Sometimes they use a series of pay phones, different ones for different times of day."

Jefferson nodded slowly. "Well, if this cockroach is able to hang around bus stations all day, waiting for the phone to ring, he can't be no hotshot spy, right? Just some sort of messenger, a go-between."

"I guess. Anyhow, it seems like the day for funny code names . . . does 'the Scalpel' mean anything to you?"

"You're the spy."

"He's an agent from Department Eight, Directorate S. Do you know what that—"

"Yeah. Assassination and sabotage. The ones who used to be Department Thirteen."

"That's right. He's been in the country for a few days. He drove across from Mexico, they found out, and then flew to Boston. Leusner thinks the KGB might have imported him for the Foley thing."

"He's really bad?"

"I guess so. Been at it over twenty years; trained a lot of Bulgarians, Libyans, Lebanese, and so on. Evidently he's the one who killed that Japanese ambassador last year. But Leusner says his specialty is getting information. Torture. Bad news for the Foleys."

"He doesn't torture people with a scalpel."

"I don't know."

"Seriously." He made a delicate gesture. "Like you don't want a fighting knife to be razor-sharp; guy doesn't even know he's been cut. A scalpel wouldn't hurt enough for torture. Lots of blood and shock. Guy you're tryin' to get to talk, he'd faint and then die."

"But suppose you could scare him enough. Lop off a finger or something."

"Nah. Somebody did that to me, I'd know he was goin' to kill me sooner or later. I wouldn't give him shit. Wouldn't make any difference."

"Not everyone's like you, Jefferson. I'd probably start thinking about the other nine fingers. Not to mention noses and ears and dicks and so forth."

"Yeah, and the Cavalry comin' over the hill. It don't happen, Bailey. Sooner or later your luck runs out and that's it. That's all she wrote."

"That's a funny thing for you to say. You've got more lives than a cat."

He stared into his glass, swirling the ice around. "Still just a matter of time. Sooner or later she comes home."

CHAPTER SIXTEEN

NICK

IT WAS TRIVIALLY easy to give myself an assignment to Boston. Jacob Bailey was told that I was a Soviet Affairs psychologist from Langley who wanted to be briefed on the Foley case, to talk informally in hopes of cross-pollination; maybe open up a new approach toward catching Foley or tracking down his captive wife.

I wanted to get a feeling for the overall operation there, since someone was obviously playing both sides. That was clear from what the Bulgarians revealed. I was sure it wasn't Jacob, since I had asked him "under the influence"; likewise, I knew that he hadn't suspected anyone at that time.

Jacob and his bodyguard, Sergeant Jefferson, picked me up at the airport and installed me in a modest hotel next to the library downtown, saying we'd get together in a couple of hours for dinner. They said Tuesday would be better than today for meeting the staff; most of them were gone on a four-day weekend, taking advantage of a package deal at a New Hampshire ski lodge. So I walked around the library for a while, feeling nostalgic, and returned to the hotel restaurant one minute early. They were waiting.

Jefferson turned out to be a more interesting man than one would expect from his profession. He'd been to a lot of the world and kept his eyes open. Those eyes had a sadness and hardness that I could identify with.

I had enjoyed Jacob's company in our previous incarnation, so perhaps I can be forgiven a large mistake. I excused myself to go to the men's room and thought nothing of it when he followed me.

We were the only ones in the facility. I was standing in a vulnerable position when I felt the cold circle of a gun muzzle against the back of my neck.

"I know that you're Foley," he said.

My heart stumbled, restarted. "Me? Foley?"

"Come on, don't be cute. Whatever you did to me in Paris, you're not going to do here. At this range even I can't miss." Through the cool metal I could feel him trembling.

"Look . . . let me take you to a doctor. The strain—"

"It's not gonna work, Foley. Your own mother wouldn't recognize you, but I do. Put your hands up, slowly."

"Let me zip up first." In the process I turned on the watch. "Give the pistol to me." He handed it over, a pearl-handled chrome-plated .25-caliber Beretta Bantam; what we used to call a "ladies' gun" in the bad old sexist days. I gave it back. "Put this away and don't ever point a gun at me again." He dropped it in the side pocket of his jacket. I wondered whether Jefferson had noticed he was armed.

"Do you usually carry a gun?"

"No, it stays in the desk drawer at home. I was afraid that you would give me trouble."

"Is this conversation being recorded or monitored?"

"I don't think so."

"How could you remember who I was?"

"It was study, not memory. There's a lot less flesh on your face, but your bone structure's the same. And your eyes, except for the colored contacts. The contacts are pretty obvious if you're looking for them."

"Have you discussed this with anyone?"

"No. It was my own little project. Besides, I'm afraid that my section has been compromised."

"Do you think anyone else is following your line of investigation?"

"I doubt it. It takes an artist's instinct. . . . I've been an amateur artist since grade school. In the past couple of months I've drawn and painted dozens of pictures, trying to guess what you might look like without the beard, or with a trimmed one. Studied hundreds of photographs. Every picture Valerie kept in her scrapbooks."

"Are those photographs in your possession now, at home?"

"No. The FBI loaned them to us; we have file copies that I borrow over the weekends."

"The paintings and drawings, are they all at home?"

"Yes, in a file folder."

"Tonight I want you to throw them all away. Forget you ever did them . . . instead, you'll remember having spent the time watching television. And you will never draw or paint a picture of me again."

"Okay."

"You will forget that you ever suspected I was Foley. If anyone else suspects that while I'm here, you will tell me immediately. And not let the other person know you've told me." He nodded. "You will follow these commands without remembering that I gave them to you. You came to the men's room because you had to urinate. After I count to three, you will use the urinal and then return to our table with me. You will remember nothing of our conversation. One . . . two . . ."

"Wait." He had a pained look.

"Yes?"

"I—I'm confused. It's as if . . . it's like I have to do anything you say."

"That's right."

"But why?"

"Three." He turned to the urinal and used it while I waited at the door. Walking back to the table, he looked puzzled. "What's wrong?"

"I don't know. Fugue state, I guess. Like my brain put in the clutch for a minute." Nervous laugh. "This Foley business, I guess. It's getting to me."

The next morning I showed up at the office at nine and met all the staff as they reported to work. One by one, I managed to get them alone and ask, with the aid of the watch, whether they passed information on to the KGB. The third, Roberta Bender, said yes. I asked her to come up to my hotel room after work, giving her the number of the extra room I'd arranged for, in case I had to talk to someone in private. I didn't think the CIA routinely bugged the rooms of visiting firemen, but this was far from being a routine case.

She knocked on the door promptly at 5:30. She was a single woman in her forties, figure well cared for, face handsome but hard under too much well-applied makeup. I had a vague sense that I'd seen her before, but wasn't sure where. She had probably picked up one of my dead drops.

I installed her in the easy chair and found my notebook, then sat on the bed across from her. "I'm going to ask you several questions. You will give me detailed answers. When I say, 'Forget this,' you will go home, have some dinner, go to bed, and sleep soundly. When you get home, you will forget having met me." She nodded. I asked whether she was being monitored, and she said no.

"Is your KGB contact Vladimir Borachev?"

"No. I know him, of course, from the office and what Jake said about their meeting. My contact is Mr. Tarakan."

Mister Cockroach. "—Do you speak Russian?"

"I didn't understand that. I don't speak Russian."

"Do you meet with Tarakan regularly?"

"I go to the statue of Samuel Eliot Morison, on Commonwealth, every other Wednesday at noon. He is often there. We walk through the Common and talk."

"Why do you do it?"

"They pay me the same as my salary, in cash."

"Patriotism or love of communism doesn't enter into it?"

"No," she said harshly. "It's a game."

"Do you know what's happened to Valerie Foley?"

"She's being held."

"Where?"

"I don't know. Tarakan said she's not in Boston anymore."

"Is she all right?"

"The last I heard, she was. But now there's this new man on her case."

"The Scalpel." Jefferson had told me about him.

"He wants to find Foley and send him one of her ears. That's worked before. Then another ear and so forth."

"They're that sure Foley wouldn't call the police?"

"They seem to be. I'm not."

"Why so?"

"They're acting as if Foley is a normal person. But he obviously isn't; he's a madman. There's no way to tell what he might do. I think he *wants* her dead. Otherwise he would have done something with whatever that power of his is."

That stopped me for a moment. Could there be truth in that? I changed the subject. "Do you have any idea why you report to Tarakan rather than Borachev?"

"I think they knew years ago that Borachev was unreliable. It certainly has turned out to be the case. Maybe everyone working under Borachev has a counterpart working with Tarakan. He's implied that."

"What has Tarakan said about Foley?"

"He doesn't say much about anything. He listens. But, let me see, he did say he expected Foley to return to Boston and that we would know when that was, unless he drives up . . . and he doesn't have a license. The FBI's watching all the airports and so forth, and we have someone pretty high up there."

"All right. Will you be meeting Tarakan tomorrow?"

"If he comes."

I was trying to remember what that area looked like. "After you meet him at the statue, do you go through the Public Garden on the way to the Common?"

"Yes, always."

"I'll meet you there. You won't show any sign of recognizing me." She nodded. "Forget this." She picked up her coat and left without a word.

So it would be soon now. Time to start carrying the gun again, or guns. I still had the small automatic I'd taken from the dope dealer the night I left Boston, as

well as the modified nine-millimeter Browning I'd
bought in Iowa long ago. I took the shoulder harness
out of my luggage and tightened up a couple of straps
to make it fit my new frame. It looked disappoint-
ingly obvious with the new suit coats; I'd long since
gotten rid of the one that had been tailored to conceal
it. When the stores opened in the morning, I would
find something.

The zippered fleece-lined jacket was bulky enough
to hide two pistols and a picnic ham besides, but it
was a little warm for the unseasonably pleasant
weather. I'd gone to a gun shop and talked the owner
out of a box of ammunition for the Browning and
four spare clips, which I had secreted in various
pockets. I was ready to take on all cockroaches and
scalpels and whatever else.

Carrying the guns made me nervous. When I'd
carried one before, it was largely a symbolic gesture.
Now I might actually have to shoot someone. I'd
been responsible for the deaths of many deserving
people, but had never pulled the trigger myself.

Squeezed the trigger. That was one thing I knew
about this business: Make the first shot count, or you
may not get a second one. I'm not an Olympic-class
marksman anymore, but I could still put a bullet into
someone's eye from across a room. Right or left eye,
take your pick. So long as my nerves hold. I held out
my hands and regretted a slight tremor.

It was hard to concentrate on the newspaper. Sitting on the park bench feeling conspicuous, over-
dressed. Hundreds of people passing by, all wondering whether I had a concealed weapon or simply
a fetish for L. L. Bean clothing. Actually, I suppose
if anyone gave it a thought, that thought was "My,
don't old geezers get cold easily." You wouldn't

call me a geezer if you knew what I had under my left armpit. Where did that word come from anyway? One who geezes.

They finally showed up, Roberta Bender with a man much shorter than she, almost a dwarf, skinny. They stood at the crosswalk, obediently waiting for the light to change. I rolled the coat's sleeve up past the watch and turned it on. Maximum gain against the traffic noise.

For some reason I had not expected it to be easy. It wasn't going to be. The first thing that went wrong was an unexpected wrinkle, something that had never happened with the watch before. As they passed me, I stood up and followed them into the Common. When there was no one within earshot, I stepped between them. "Tarakan," I said, "will you answer some questions for me?"

"All right," he said.

"What?" Bender said. "Who is this man? Don't tell him anything!"

"All right," he said again.

"Shut up, Roberta. Don't say another word until I'm gone." She nodded. "Tarakan, what's your real name?"

"I cannot tell you anything."

"Yes, you can. She didn't know what she was saying. You can talk to me. What is your name?"

He looked from her to me and made a strangled noise. Absolute orders that conflicted. I turned to Bender. "Tell him to answer me." She made a similar strangled noise. With my careless syntax, I had effectively silenced both of them!

Start over. "All right. Both of you forget everything that's happened in the past sixty seconds."

They both gave a little stagger. "Who are you?" Bender demanded.

"A friend. You will both answer all of my questions." They nodded. "Let's walk." I asked the cockroach what his real name was; he said Igor Melentev. I wrote it down.

"Igor, where is Valerie Foley being held?"

"Someplace in the Washington area. All I have is a phone number."

"Give it to me."

"I don't have it memorized. It's back at my apartment." He gave me the address, a fairly sleazy area near Chinatown. We walked to a cabstand, and I had us delivered to a location a few blocks from Igor's place.

It was a good area for a cockroach to live in. Triple-X theaters and massage parlors. Sidewalks more slept on than swept. Everywhere the excrement of large dogs. One hoped.

He rented the second-floor loft of a tenement that was otherwise used only as a warehouse. We had to edge single-file through the vestibule, which was stacked high with dusty boxes, and inch carefully up the unlit stairs. The air was mildew and mold and damp concrete.

He unlocked the door to his loft and fluorescent lights flicked into momentarily blinding brilliance. The large room was neat and spare, mostly empty space. Cot, chair, desk, filing cabinet clustered at one end of a thousand square feet of brown indoor-outdoor carpet. No bookcase, radio, television; no real sense of habitation.

"It's over here." He led us to the desk, set down his glasses, and opened the drawer. He pulled a Colt Woodsman with a homemade silencer and pointed it at my face. "Who are you?"

"Put that gun away," I said.

"That won't work." Without looking away from

me he touched his glasses. "These glasses have a built-in hearing aid. It has been working only intermittently today. I find that when I can hear clearly, I have to do what you say. That must be Foley's secret weapon. You work for him, don't you?"

"Yes, I do."

"Then you're just the one we've been waiting for. Roberta, come here. There's some strapping tape in the bottom drawer. Tie him up."

So I was not the only careless person in the room. When she came up beside him, I said, *"Take the gun!"*—and she made a grab for it.

He got off one shot before she grasped the weapon. The report was like a cap pistol; the bullet whirred past my ear. Then two more wild shots, one ricocheting crazily, while he struggled with the large woman, and then I had the Browning out, one loud blast. The center of his nose blossomed and his head rocked back, spraying brains. He staggered sideways and fell across the desk with a horrible groan. Roberta was screaming at the top of her lungs. I got a good sight picture between her eyes but didn't shoot. *"Shut up!"* I yelled, twice. The second time, she was inhaling and heard me. She quieted but continued to pant and whimper, staring at the dying body as it rustled and spilled. She was trying to cram her fist into her mouth.

I checked to make sure there were no blood spots on her clothing and led her to the door. "When you go out of this door, you will forget everything that has happened since meeting Tarakan today. You will go home, call in sick, and sleep for the rest of the day." I opened the door and gently pushed her out.

Speed. There was an address book in the drawer from which he'd taken the gun. I pocketed it and then dumped everything on the floor; try to make it look like a burglary. I took his wallet and the silenced pistol. Wiped my fingerprints off drawer handles and ran out the door and down the dark stairs, almost breaking my neck on the last one. Went down the musty hall to a back entrance and stepped out into an alley. No sirens. Not a sound; no sign of life. Perhaps a single gunshot was not that much of a novelty here. Without hurrying, I walked to the Washington Street T stop and took the subway back to my hotel.

That was when the reaction set in. I almost fainted in the elevator. I just managed to get inside the room, where I fell on the bed fully clothed and shook for several minutes.

Then I called Room Service and asked for a double brandy. Locked all the armaments in the closet and took a quick hot-cold-shower. I was just finished dressing when the drink came. I tipped the boy more than the drink cost and, as soon as the door closed, drank half of it in a gulp. Then I sat to sip at it and leaf through the address book, on the off chance that he had been telling the truth.

He evidently was. There were no names, just initials—but only one number had the Washington area code, 202.

CHAPTER SEVENTEEN

VALERIE

HE LET ME think about that razor blade and his prestidigitation for two days. I received nothing but water for those two days and, with the exception of bathroom breaks, was kept handcuffed to the chair the whole time. It did give me time to think, though it was hard to think of anything constructive.

I wondered who was taking my classes. Where Nick was. What kind of winter it had been. Where the police were. How long they were going to keep me alive. Where the FBI was. How my parents were taking it. Where the CIA was. Where Nick was.

And over and over, why did they want Nick so badly? He obviously hadn't told me everything. Was that just spy-stuff secrecy, or was it something so terrible he thought I couldn't handle it? Or couldn't be trusted.

The woman who was watching me left, and the fat man came back, moving with the same weird, silent grace as before. Staring at me. "What's your name?" I asked, to break the spell.

He sat down and smiled. "The CIA has been calling me the Scalpel, which is funny. I've never used a scalpel."

"Just that razor blade."

"No, that was a new one. Never used." He set a heavy pistol on the table. "Do you know where this comes from?"

"Is it Nick's?"

"Yes. So let us have no foolishness about him not being involved with guns."

"But that's a target pistol, isn't it? He used to coach—"

"Yes, it is a target pistol. It's also the weapon of choice for most assassinations performed by organized crime. They should know what works best, don't you think?"

"Nick could never murder anybody."

"We know differently. You know differently."

"You're wrong. I've know him since . . ."

He leaned across the table and slowly began unbuttoning my blouse. I shrank away, but the chair was bolted to the floor. "You're going to add sexual battery to kidnapping?" I asked.

"It would make no difference, would it? In terms of punishment." He undid the last button and spread the blouse open. I wasn't wearing a bra. "But no, I'm not interested in you . . . that way. Though I compliment you on having kept your shape. Handball, is it?"

"Yes."

"And self-defense, your dossier says; one reason you're kept handcuffed." He continued to inspect me, with a pouty kind of smile. He had the lips of a fat baby.

"So what's the point in undressing me? I'm beyond being embarrassed. If you want to see my body, you can come in while I'm bathing. I certainly can't stop you." Actually, only the female guard had been with me in the bathroom, and always with eyes averted.

He produced a cigarette from the air and lit it care-fully with a wooden match. It was one of those thick French cigarettes with the yellow paper. It smelled like compost burning. He squinted at me through the rising fumes.

He moved the cigarette to the corner of his mouth by a sensual rolling of the lips. "I also know that your academic specialty is abnormal psychology. Perhaps you can help me. With a personal problem."

"Go ahead."

"Some thirty years ago, I was castrated."

"My God. I'm sorry."

"Don't be. It was done with anesthesia."

"By the State?"

"In a sense," he said, or perhaps "in essence." He glanced around for an ashtray and, finding none, gently rolled the ash of his cigarette onto the tabletop. "It was an internal-security measure by the KGB, perhaps not sanctioned by the Party. I agreed to the operation."

"Rather than die."

"That was the implication. Let me explain." He stood up and walked a couple of paces away, and spoke with his back to me.

"When I was younger, I was a sadist. I mean that in the precise clinical way: a person who can only be sexually aroused by inflicting pain on his partner."

My heart started to hammer. Could he be making this up to scare me?

"I grew up on a farm. My first sexual encounters were with animals. Once a sheep tried to get away from me, and I killed it. The blood was . . . exciting beyond expression. I made it a practice. Hurting them, sometimes killing them.

"When I was older, after Stalin, I sought out partners who did not mind pain, or enjoyed it. Most of them were other young men, though I preferred women. Older women. I would have liked you." I was not especially grateful.

"I was accepted by the MGB, which was one of the KGB's predecessors, and after a couple of years they posted me to Germany. That was a godsend, since prostitutes there were often amenable to sadism, and there was no . . . political problems. In Russia I was often afraid that one of my partners would exploit our relationship.

"After a few years, though, my superiors evidently got suspicious. I hired a prostitute from my usual source. As it turned out, she was actually one of our agents from another city. She played the part with enthusiasm. But once she had ample evidence of my proclivities, she revealed who she was and ordered me to stop. It was bad timing on her part. As much out of anger as desire, I killed her. She was the only one I ever killed. Of course I wasn't able to cover it up.

"But for various reasons I was valuable to the NKVD. So I was allowed to be castrated as an experiment in . . . attitude adjustment. What do you think of that?"

"I don't know what to think. I hope it's a fantasy you're using in order to scare—"

"No." He turned around and slowly exposed himself: crotch as featureless as a plastic doll's. Catheter and bag, no penis. As he methodically redressed, he continued. "So I am no longer a sadist in the strictest sense of the word. My only sexual activity is a periodic shot of testosterone, to prevent glandular imbalance.

"However, I find I do still take a sort of detached pleasure in inflicting pain. And I know a great deal about people's reactions to pain." He leaned over the table toward me. The burning cigarette was about a foot from my bare chest.

"If you're trying to frighten me," I said, "you've succeeded. I'll tell you anything you want to know." The quaver in my voice was genuine. "I'm no hero, heroine."

"That is a problem." He moved the cigarette closer; I could feel the heat from its ember on my left breast. "People *will* tell you whatever they think you want to hear. Rather than the truth."

The chair back creaked with the force of my retreat from the coal, as he brought it to within an inch of the nipple. I closed my eyes tight and even so had to turn away. A crawling, tingling sensation raced up and down my back; my guts churned. "I'm going to be sick," I said through clenched jaws.

"Not very. You haven't eaten in two days." But he took the cigarette away. I opened my eyes and saw him take a long drag on it and then drop it and grind it out on the floor. He had a grotesque, earnest expression.

"Do you understand?" he said quietly. "I can cause you so much pain that even after it stops, you will want to die rather than live with the memory of it." He began to button up my blouse. "And I can withhold death indefinitely."

He straightened my collar and touched my cheek with his warm, dry hand. "I hope you can see that it is an impersonal process. I am a technician charged with extracting reliable information. What's at stake is so important that whether you live or die, or whether I do, means absolutely nothing. Your happiness or agonies are meaningless. Do you understand?"

"What is at stake?"

He stabbed with a thumbnail, not hard, at a pressure point under my cheekbone. It caused an electrifying spark of pain, like the dentist touching a nerve. "I asked whether you understood."

"Yes. I do." What did I know about sadism that I could possibly use as a defense? What could anybody know that would apply to this man's bizarre case?

"It could be that *everything* is at stake. Your husband is a wild card. He even has the CIA terrified."

"That sounds incredible."

"The KGB is not happy with him, either. While he was in Paris, he killed two agents assigned to interrogate him."

"They must have done something awful."

"Your loyalty is touching. But as far as we can tell, they did nothing out of the ordinary. Certainly nothing like what you are going through."

"I see." I could go through rather less and cheerfully kill anyone responsible.

"The *way* he killed them is especially interesting. One of them lived long enough to describe it, and that's what has the CIA and the KGB upset. It interests me, personally, very much." He paused.

I didn't know what sort of response was expected, or safe. "Because?"

"Because he didn't lay a hand on them. He said something to them. Then they took a long train ride, got off at the end of the line, walked out into the country, and killed each other. Rather, one killed the other and then shot himself in the head. Now, don't you think that's remarkable?"

"Uh, yes."

"Does it remind you of anything?" My mind was a blank. What was I supposed to say? Don't hurt me? "Come on, now. It must remind you of something." He walked around to stand behind me, out of sight. "What could it be?"

"A . . . movie?"

He put his left hand in my hair and wove his fingers through it tightly, barely painful, immobilizing my head. "Something to do with your husband."

"Just that . . . he caused it, you said?"

He pinched behind my earlobe with his thumbnail and began increasing pressure. "A process. The name of a process."

"I can't think when you—"

"What do you call it," he said, suddenly increasing pressure with both hands, "when you induce a trance in a person and tell him to do something?"

"Hypnosis!" I cried through the blinding pain.

"Very good." He kept up the pressure for a few seconds and then slowly let go. He walked back around and sat down. Took out a Kleenex and dabbed at my tears. "You see? You *can* think while I'm hurting you. It's up to you to convince me that you think better when I'm not. Do you understand?"

"I understand."

"Tell me about your husband and hypnotism."

"But he couldn't have hypnotized those men and ordered them . . . nobody could—"

"I know. Tell me anyhow. Everything."

That was a long time ago. "One winter, before we were married, he was very interested in it. We practiced on each other. I was a better subject—"

"Or he was a better hypnotist?"

"That could be. We didn't think so at the time. Just that some people are hard to hypnotize."

"All right. Go on."

Suddenly a memory rushed in, and I tried hard to suppress it. It's difficult to think about one thing and talk about another. "He wrote a paper about it."

"I've read the paper. It doesn't seem particularly relevant."

The time I started undressing. *Don't think about it!*
He said something to me *don't* and I started stripping
don't think right there in the laboratory. "I don't,
don't think he, uh, wrote any other papers."

"Valerie." He reached over and patted my right
hand. "I told you, I do this for a living. You are
withholding information." He bent my little finger
back almost to the breaking point. "I will break your
finger. Then I will break the next one, and the next."

"Please. No." Tears dripping, trying not to scream.

He suddenly relaxed his grip. "I want you to think
very hard over the next twenty-four hours. Recall all
that you can about your husband and hypnotism. If I
am satisfied with your testimony, your fingers . . . stay
unbroken."

He stood up and walked toward the door. "If not, I
will break one finger each hour." At the door, he
looked back down the long room at me. "After ten
hours, I will do more serious damage. The blade."

He smiled and closed the door silently behind him.
When had I wet myself?

CHAPTER EIGHTEEN

JACOB

FOLEY MAY BE back in Boston. At least one of his guns is.

The police called in the FBI when they came across some suspicious-looking documents, investigating a rather gruesome break-in/murder down by the Combat Zone. The papers turned out to be computer listings for some highly classified General Dynamics software; the aiming system for a new antisatellite particle-beam weapon. So we were brought in on it.

The man was shot once in the head with a nine-millimeter automatic. The picture of the scene of the crime reminded me of that unlucky Bulgarian agent. I would like to go a long time without seeing another head wound.

Anyhow, the FBI retrieved the bullet from the wall behind the body and checked the rifling on it. Put it through their computer and, as too rarely happens, actually did identify the weapon. It belonged to Nicholas Foley. (Twenty years ago Foley had the weapon "accuratized" by a Nebraska gunsmith, by mail. The gunsmith kept a file of sample bullets from each customer and periodically sent them to the FBI.)

Of course, the KGB could have stolen the weapon when they broke in to kidnap Mrs. Foley. We know from a previous clandestine search that Foley owned at least two pistols, a .22 target pistol and the accuratized Browning, and they were both gone after the kidnapping. Since Foley never went back to the apartment, if he still has the Browning, then he would have had to carry it to Paris with him. Or stash it at the airport. Either one is possible, but I suppose it's about equally likely that the murder was an internal KGB affair. They may have used Foley's pistol to confuse us—though in that case you would think they would have left it at the scene—or possibly just used it because it was handy.

It wasn't a simple execution. The man had powder residue on his right hand. He evidently had fired at least three rounds from a .22, which went in three different directions. Was he shooting at three different assailants? Struggling? The police say that if he was struggling, it wasn't with the person who shot him. From the angle of fire and the position of the spent cartridge case, they can tell that the assailant was about eight feet away.

So it's possible that Foley has an accomplice, or several. It could be anybody, and it could be a temporary arrangement. Evidently he can walk up to anybody and say, "Pardon me, but would you mind helping me murder a Russian spy?" and have them pull the trigger and then forget about it afterward.

There was no real witness, unfortunately. An anonymous caller gave the address and said she had heard a shot. That's more cooperation than the police normally expect in the Zone.

Anyhow, we're assuming that Foley is in Boston. The police and FBI are weaving a pretty tight net. Maybe this time.

CHAPTER NINETEEN

NICK

I WAS OUT of Boston before the cockroach's body was cold. Packed my small suitcase and in a half hour was at the station, waiting for the first train south. With the watch turned up high, I called Jacob's office and talked to each person, fixing. On the train, sat in the bar car and drank too much warm Budweiser. When I got back to my Georgetown apartment, I collapsed and slept for twelve hours.

The telephone number in his address book was unlisted, but I didn't have any trouble getting the address from Ma Bell. A suite in the Watergate Hotel, probably not where Valerie was being held. At nine o'clock I called the suite and told the person who answered, in Russian, that I was from Moscow, an associate of Tarakan's, and would meet him in one hour on the steps of the JFK Center. He asked if something was wrong, and I said, *"Da."*

He was a nervous young man, constantly fingering the red rose in his lapel. I'd asked him to wear a flower for identification. After watching him for a while, to see whether his glance or posture would betray knowledge of a third person's presence, I finally walked up to him and shook hands.

"Let's go down to the river," I suggested before he could suggest otherwise. We walked out and crossed the street. The fleece-lined jacket was a comfort, not just because of the armament it concealed. The temperature had started dropping at ten o'clock; there was blizzard in the air. The wind off the Potomac was vicious. I turned the watch's gain up all the way.

"After you called, I tried to reach Tarakan," the young man said. "He wasn't at the proper number."

"There's trouble. I went to see him yesterday, and there were police cars everywhere. I thought it would be well to leave Boston for a while."

"Probably wise. We can get a *Globe* at the hotel newsstand and see what it says."

We got to the edge of the water and turned to walk with our backs to the wind. "How was Tarakan involved with this Foley thing?"

"He just started about two weeks ago. He was the one who suggested we bring in *gospodin* Shilkov." The Scalpel. He shivered, not from the cold. "He more than suggested it."

"You don't approve of Shilkov?"

"I can't even look at him, his eyes. Knowing what I know."

"Which is?"

"He can't wait to torture her. Torture her and then kill her. That's the way he is, the monster."

"Has he—"

"—We don't have to *do* this!" the man continued, in Russian, with emotion. "—It just brings us down to their level! *Beneath* their level! Murder and kidnapping, torture. We should have exposed everything about the Bulgarian incident and compelled the Americans to explain it. Imagine the embarrassment to—"

"Has he hurt her?"

"Not yet, not that I've heard. He's supposed to exhaust all normal techniques of interrogation first."

"Where are they?"

"An unused factory building in Cabin John, Maryland." Just across the river from Langley! "It's right at the township limits, Two hundred North Carroll Drive."

"How many are there?"

"It varies. Always at least three guards, one with her and two outside. And Shilkov, I think he's staying there."

"Do you have a car?"

"Yes."

"Take me there, now." I wasn't thinking clearly. I should have asked one more question.

Snow had started to fall by the time we got his car out of the lot and pointed in the right direction. We'd be going within a few blocks of my apartment, and I was tempted to stop by and pick up the second gun. But I decided that it would be better to arrive a few minutes earlier, especially if the snow got worse. If one gun didn't do the trick, then two probably wouldn't be any better.

Before we were out of Georgetown, the snow was falling and blowing so hard that I could barely see the car in front of us. The driver hunched over the wheel and gave short answers to my questions.

"How long has Mrs. Foley been here?"

"Month."

"Where was she before that?"

"Boston, I guess."

"They didn't tell you?"

"No."

"What is your job in connection with her?"

"Guard, sometimes. Shopping."

"Are you armed?"

"No. Gun's at the place, the factory."

"Where at the factory?" Just in case.

"Table in the prisoner's room. By the door."

"What keeps the prisoner from taking it?"

"She can't go anywhere. Handcuffed to a chair that's bolted to the floor."

"Are there other weapons?"

"Probably."

"Elaborate on that, please."

"Shilkov always has a gun. And there's a locked closet. Shilkov has the key. He said we didn't need to know what was in it."

We drove along in silence for a few minutes. "I don't understand," he said, "why I have to answer all your questions. Why I'm driving you out here through the snow."

"Don't worry about it."

"All right." But a mile later, he persisted. "I've seen pictures of Foley. You aren't him, are you? In disguise?"

"No. I work for him." Might as well plant some misdirection. "I'm a private detective he hired in Boston. I haven't seen him in over a month. Hope he's still alive."

"He hired you to find Mrs. Foley?"

"That's right. Half the money up front, half if I deliver her." He nodded. "Do you feel sorry for her?"

"Yes, of course."

"Elaborate."

"They say she's not one of us, an innocent by-stander. If she has to die in this war, I wish it could be without torment."

"What war do you feel you are fighting? What aims?"

He thought for a moment. "First, to contain American imperialism and militarism. Second, to encourage the growth of humane Communist leadership in contested parts of the world. The two are related, of course."

Not so different from what I would have said at his age. I suddenly felt old and tired. "Look. I have a secret word for you."

"Yes?"

"When I say the word *kumquat*, I want you to do everything in your power to subdue Shilkov. Even if you have to kill him."

He nodded slowly. "I think I can do that."

We drove the rest of the way to Cabin John in silence. North Carroll Road turned out to be little more than a bulldozed strip of frozen mud, and number 200 was the only building on it. It was a half-finished factory building, evidently a project that had run out of money. We parked in front and got out. There were no other buildings in sight, and to the rear of the factory a public dump supplied an interesting odor.

We opened the door and there were two men with two guns. No chance. The short fat one laughed, said "Kumquat," and fired a shot from a large pistol. The driver screamed, and a second shot cut off the scream. At the same time, before I could even reach inside my coat, the other man, kneeling with a rifle, shot me in the chest.

CHAPTER TWENTY

VALERIE

I THOUGHT THIS was going to be it for sure. The door banged open, and the Scalpel strode in with a bright smile, bright eyes. Looking forward to something, presumably hurting me. All he did, though, was unlock the handcuffs, slide me onto the floor, and then reattach the cuffs to the chair leg. I found my voice. "What's happening?"

He laughed his one-syllable laugh. "Company coming. A gentleman your husband hired." He went back into the anteroom, and I overheard him arguing with a couple of the guards. They went outside, and I heard a car drive away. So I was left with just the Scalpel and his little buddy, Sam. Sam was the only American there, and I think he wanted to grow up to be like the Scalpel. When he stood guard over me, it was with a wistful smile and bad thoughts radiating.

The two of them left me alone. After a few minutes a car pulled up outside, one I hadn't heard before. The outside door opened, and the Scalpel said something I didn't understand. Then there were two loud gunshots, with a scream in between.

They came back in carrying a limp body between them, a man with a pillowcase pulled over his head.

They slid the table aside, heaved him onto my chair, and handcuffed him to the armrests—and then I realized it was Nick! He must have lost seventy pounds. But he still wore the wedding ring I gave him, and the fancy Italian shoes he'd treated himself to last birthday.

"Now take your place with the rifle, Sam." The Scalpel rummaged through the table drawer and brought out a hypodermic needle. He inspected it, squirted out a small amount of clear fluid. Sam disappeared, then returned to the other end of the room with a strange-looking rifle, and seated himself in a chair. The Scalpel rolled up Nick's coat sleeve and gave him an injection in the wrist.

After a moment Nick shifted his weight, sitting forward, and shook his head under the pillowcase.

"Listen carefully," the Scalpel said. "You were shot with a tranquilizing dart, a powerful drug that puts a person to sleep almost instantly. I've given you an antidote. The rifleman who shot you is in this room, but far out of your reach. If you do anything suspicious, you will be shot again. I don't think that would be good for your health. Do you understand?"

He cleared his throat and swallowed. "I understand." It wasn't Nick's voice at all.

"The agent you captured was wearing a very sensitive microphone; we could hear your very breath. We know exactly who you are and why you've come. First, where is Foley?"

"I don't know. He was going to contact me in Boston, next week." I pinned it down then. Nick always had a talent for mimicry; he was using the voice of Larry Martino, his department head. "He didn't tell me anything else."

"I don't believe that. Second, what is the origin of this power you and he can use?"

"A drug. Foley told me the name; I can't pronounce it. Or remember it, actually. Poly something. Maybe he ordered me not to be able to remember the name."

"I don't believe that, either. Do you have any of the drug with you?"

"No, I used it all on the man from Watergate."

"How did you get him to swallow it?"

"I didn't. It's an aerosol."

"So many things I don't believe. We're going to start over. Try to visualize this. The woman you were sent to rescue is handcuffed to the chair you're sitting in. I have a razor blade in my hand. The next time I don't believe an answer, I will slash her face. Where is Foley?"

"He's bluffing," I said desperately. He kneeled down and pinned my shoulder with his crushing left-hand grip and waved the blade inches over my face. I gasped.

"Don't harm her!" Nick said in his real voice, thick with emotion. The Scalpel eased back and looked at the razor blade with a strange expression.

"So that's all . . . you just . . . Sam—"

"Get between me and the rifleman," Nick said quickly, too quietly for Sam to hear. The Scalpel did as he said. "Now take the razor and slash your own wrist." He did, and stared openmouthed at the rush of blood.

"What's going on there, Misha?" Sam said. "I can't—"

"Drop the razor and shoot the rifleman. Kill him." The Scalpel jerked a pistol out of his pocket and spun around. A dart hit him in the shoulder, and at the same time he fired two fast, loud shots. Sam flung the rifle away, and his chair tipped over. "Valerie, stay calm." The involuntary scream that was gathering disappeared.

"Now give the gun to Valerie and then pick up the razor and cut your own throat. You bastard." But he was beyond obeying, staggering from the drug. He dropped the gun and fell on top of it.

"He got hit by a dart," I said. "I guess you won't get anything more out of him."

"Can you reach the gun?"

"No; it's underneath him."

"Damn. What about the rifleman?"

"I think he's dead. He's not moving."

"Okay." He thought for a moment. "Can you stand up far enough to use your teeth to get this thing off my head?"

"I'll try." He leaned over as far as he could, and I was able to slide the pillowcase off. "What . . ." At first I didn't recognize him; clean-shaven, gaunt, suntanned. "No wonder they thought you were someone else."

"Overhearing helped. The car must have been bugged." He made a familiar head gesture, and we kissed. It felt strange. Then he studied the Scalpel's body. "He must have keys. Let me see." He stretched as far as he could, but his toe stopped a few inches short. "See if you can reach him. If we could get the pistol . . ."

I could just get a toe under his hip. But I couldn't budge his heavy body. "I'm too weak," I said, tears starting. "I've been sitting in that chair forever—"

"Listen. You can do it. Use your toe and flip him over." Incredibly, I did. His left arm, flopping, trailed an arc of bright-red drops. My calf immediately seized up with a cramp, and I cried out.

"Sorry, dear. Ignore the pain." It went away. "Now slide the pistol over to where you can pick it up." I

did. "Now shoot away the chain on this right handcuff. Aim down the room and look away when you
pull the trigger. Good." The shot made my ears ring
and intensified the smell of gunsmoke. I looked back,
and it had worked, after a fashion. Nick was grimac-
ing, holding his wrist against his chest. The side of
his hand was bleeding. "Chain bounced up," he said.
"Let me have the gun." He pulled the other chain
tight, told me to look away, and blasted it. Then he
jumped out of the chair and knelt by the Scalpel. He
put the pistol to the man's head.

"Please don't," I said weakly. "Enough is
enough."

"He may live."

"Please."

"All right." He went through the Scalpel's pockets
and came up with another pistol, which he tucked
into his shoulder holster, and a ring of keys. He unlocked me and then I undid the shot-off vestiges of
his 'cuffs.

"I thought there were two other guards," he said.

"I guess the Scalpel sent them away. They had an
argument, in Russian, and then I heard a car leave."

"Just as soon be gone before they get back." He
looked through the keys and held out one with a
Volkswagen symbol. "This must belong to the Rabbit
out front. You up to driving through the snow?"

"Nicky, I couldn't drive across a parking lot. I
can't even hold my arms up." I demonstrated. "Can
you do the rest of me like the leg?"

"Don't like to overdo it. Sooner or later you pay
for it." He chewed on a nail. "We'd better, though.
You've got so much more experience driving." He
closed his eyes and took a deep breath. "Listen:
You're plenty strong enough to drive and to walk un-
assisted. When we sit down on the airplane, you'll

fall asleep and your body will recuperate." He opened his eyes and looked at me expectantly.

I tried to lift my arms again; the muscles were still water. "I don't know. Doesn't feel any different."

"That's funny." He looked at his watch. "Oh no. Oh shit. The handcuff, the chain, must've . . ." He held his wrist out to me. So his watch was broken, big deal.

A car door slammed outside.

CHAPTER TWENTY-ONE

NICK

I CHECKED THE clip in the Browning and worked a round into the chamber. "Stay here," I said to Valerie and then realized that she probably couldn't walk without help. I was moving slowly, too, because of the drugs, and feeling dizzy and nauseated. I got to the anteroom just as the door to the outside was opening and held the pistol in a shaky two-handed "combat" grip. A woman stepped through the door, quietly talking to a man close behind her.

"Freeze!" I shouted, and added in Russian, "—Come forward slowly with your hands high." Neither of them tried anything aggressive. They stared at the carnage for a moment and obeyed.

The Watergate man had been hit in the chest and the head, leaving a colorful mess on the white door. They had to step over him and into a pool of blood. They walked into the long room and stopped. The rifleman had been shot twice in the chest; a purple stain of blood the size of a bedsheet spread down toward a drain in the floor. It seemed like more than one person's worth of blood. "—Your Misha did all this," I said.

"—*Our* Misha," the woman said. "—Misha be-

141

longs only to himself. And his work." Misha, or
Shilkov, or the Scalpel, was still adding his own con-
tribution of blood to the gruesome scene, now a slow
trickle. "—He is dead?"

"—I don't think so, not yet. We can hope." I motioned them toward the chair.

"—You are Foley's detective?" she asked.

"—That's correct."

"—Tell him that most of us regret these . . . dev-
elopments. The wrong people were empowered to
make decisions, we think, and once implemented,
they could not be undone."

"These two are all right," Valerie said. "Please
don't hurt them."

"*Spasibo,*" the man said. "Thank you."

"—Take off your coats and empty your pockets
onto the table." Be silly to handcuff them if they
could just pull out keys. "—Now sit on either side of
the chair." I kept them covered while Valerie joined
them wrist-to-wrist through the chair's legs.

I had to help Valerie to her feet. I draped the
woman's coat around her and half-carried her out to
the car. The sight of the anteroom gave her a minute
of dry heaves.

She looked around at the swirling snow and the
strange landscape. "Is this Boston?"

I told her where we were. "Strangely enough, I've
been within a few miles of here for a month, trying to
track you down. Working with the CIA across the
river."

"You've come over to their side, then? Our side."

"No, it's not like that. They thought I was someone else." I helped her into the car. "I infiltrated, to
find out whether it was them or the KGB who had
kidnapped you."

"The CIA *kidnaps* people?"

"God knows." I went around to the driver's side and got in. The car started with difficulty and stalled as soon as I let out the clutch. I started to pump the accelerator.

"Don't flood it, Nicky. We don't want to spend all day here." I followed her directions, got it going, and slithered away.

Our lives were probably in as much danger from my driving as they had been from the Scalpel's razor blade. The road crews hadn't come out this far, and although the rear-engined car was able to keep moving through the mess, it fishtailed constantly, and three times it turned completely around in slow, lazy circles. The third time ended with a bone-rattling collision, crashing my side against an abandoned car. It did a lot of damage to the other one. I left the scene of the accident rather than face a traffic cop with no license, no registration, and various people's fresh blood spattered all over my clothes.

It got a little easier once we crossed the District Line. Salt and sand on the roads. A lot of snarled traffic, though; it took over an hour to get to Georgetown. I double-parked in front of my apartment. Since my door wouldn't open, Valerie had to get out by herself, which was painful for both of us and excruciatingly slow. I got her into the apartment and onto the couch, then went out and parked the car in the closest illegal space I could find. I hadn't thought to change clothes and didn't want to be in public any longer than necessary, looking like an assassin in need of drycleaning.

We couldn't stay in the apartment for very long either, of course. Just gather resources and make plans. I put out some sardines and crackers; Valerie finished the whole plate while I was fixing tea. We switched to peanut butter, which nearly exhausted the pantry. (Valerie was surprised there was so little, since I'm a fanatic cook at home. But I'd found out that with no one else to cook for, I either ate out or just grabbed a handful of something.)

I'd fortunately stashed away a wad of twenties, emergency money. It came to four hundred dollars, and I had about fifty in my wallet. That would get us pretty far away. I cursed my stupidity at not gathering the money of the dead men and captives—but then I was used to simply asking people to hand over their wallets.

I left Valerie to look over the travel section of the paper I'd bought on the train down, to find out how far we could get for the least money, while I went into the bedroom to pack a suitcase. It was mostly a matter of indiscriminately emptying out the closet and drawers, since I had come here with one large suitcase of clothes and hadn't added much. I wrapped both pistols and their ammunition in the lead film bag and set them in the middle of the nondescript suitcase. They sometimes would conduct spot-check X-ray inspections of luggage that's checked through, I'd been told.

The tea and food had given Valerie some color. She was sitting up straight, studying the paper. "So where will it be?" I asked her.

She folded the paper and set it beside her. "First explain to me why we don't just go across the river. Go to the CIA with everything. Take them to that place while the blood's still fresh."

"It doesn't work like that. Just because the KGB are bad guys doesn't mean the CIA are good guys."

"*Tor*ture, Nicky! Bloody murder. The CIA doesn't do that routinely."

"Neither do...does the KGB. Routinely. But

there's something going on here that's even more important. More dangerous."

"Your power. That watch."

I shushed her. "Once we're someplace where I know we can't possibly be bugged, I'll tell you everything."

She tossed the newspaper onto the coffee table. "Miami, then. Two-week special; it'd cost us more to fly to Boston. I assume we want to be far away from there."

"That's right. They have a whole team on the lookout there."

She stretched and made a face. "God, I hate Florida."

CHAPTER TWENTY-TWO

JACOB

FOLEY WAS RIGHT here. He was in this office. Jefferson and I took him to dinner. How can we fight someone like this?

Roberta Bender was the key. I mentioned the guy from Langley, James Norwood, and she drew a complete blank. I knew she'd met him; the only time she hadn't been in the office during his visit was the half-day sick leave she took the day after he supposedly left. She couldn't remember anything that happened between leaving for lunch and calling in sick, a gap of a couple of hours. So she was probably with him and was told to forget. Did she witness the murder?

I asked that she volunteer for deep hypnosis, with drugs, to try to recapture as much as possible. She agreed, but wanted to rest up for a while, since besides being under the weather from flu, she still felt rattled and apprehensive over having been so eerily manipulated and was in no hurry to duplicate the experience.

After three days of not hearing from her, we went to her apartment and broke in. I'd half-expected to find her body, the result of an injunction to commit suicide rather than betray Foley. Instead we found an apartment that was more than empty: It looked as if no one had ever lived there. A salesman's model.

We brought in the FBI, and they confirmed that the place had been "cleaned" by experts. Not a finger-print, not a hair. No human skin had ever touched the sheets or pillowcases.

They said it was unlikely that one person without special equipment and training could have done so thorough a job. They suggested that if we really wanted to get in touch with Roberta Bender, we should inquire through the Soviet embassy.

So we have to assume that everything we know about Foley, the KGB knows as well. Plus whatever they've managed to extract from Mrs. Foley.

I gathered all the staff into the meeting room, and we compared notes. It wasn't very helpful. We all agreed he had looked exactly like Robert Redford, and that was about all anybody remembered.

I called Langley and talked to his section chief, who also recalled that he looked exactly like Robert Redford. Of course they had a photograph on file; he would call Personnel and have them send a copy to us. Then he called back a few minutes later to say that the photograph was missing from their records. Somehow that didn't surprise me.

I called the Society for Ethical Hypnotism and got the name of the best forensic hypnotist in New England, Laura Wentworth. We pushed through a Secret clearance for her and told her enough so that she could appreciate the need for absolute silence on the matter. Then she put me into a hypnotic state and interrogated me.

She said I was a good subject; I could recall events of the past days and months with remarkable accuracy and completeness. But when it came to Nicholas Foley, a.k.a. James Norwood, we got nowhere.

She went through the same questions while my hypnotic state was deepened with drugs, and the answers were essentially the same, if harder to understand. About all I could remember was that we had had dinner together, the conversation being mostly small talk about Boston, and he stayed in the office the next day studying the Foley files and talking with the staff. And he looked just like Robert Redford.

CHAPTER TWENTY-THREE

VALERIE

NICK WANTED TO drive us to the airport, because it would take forever to get a cab. If we waited too long, the place would be bristling with armed spies of every stripe. I vetoed him. We hadn't gone through all that just to die in a pileup in Washington traffic. Besides, all the really dangerous spies were incapacitated—handcuffed or unconscious or dead. The cab only took twenty minutes to get to us, anyhow.

At National, Nick managed to find me a skycap with a wheelchair, and we got aboard the plane without incident. He was doubly nervous in the airport for not being able to reach his guns, but he relaxed once the plane started moving. I couldn't. I alternated between fitful sleep and nauseated wakefulness all the way. Somehow I managed to keep down the sardines he had fed me and even ate the inside out of a ghastly Eastern Airlines mystery-meat sandwich. Hunger is the best sauce.

The main trick was to try not to think about the recent past. House plans and decorating ideas, course outlines and old erotic fantasies—anything but that evil man and his handcuffs and razor blade, the constant pain and weariness and anxiety, the sudden ex-

plosions of blood and . . . think about anything else. I
read the first paragraphs of many magazine articles.

My vision of Florida was a mosaic of gaudy com-
mercialism, rapacious overdevelopment, adolescent
sexuality, senescence, crime, racism, sunburn, and
cheap orange-blossom perfume. I'd been there once
and wasn't happy about the prospect of a second
time.

This time, though, the weather contrast was almost
enough to make me glad to be there. To go in a couple of hours from a slushy blizzard nightmare, cars
playing Dodg'em for keeps, to palm fronds swaying
in a warm breeze against a cobalt sky, can make up at
least for orange-blossom perfume.

Nick installed me in a coffee shop with a pile of
carbohydrates and went off in search of a paper. I was
starting to get some strength back; didn't need a
wheelchair so long as I could hold his arm.

It was good to be able to hold him again. But he
had a lot of explaining to do.

"Here you go." He handed me the classified section of the *Herald* and sat down with a tabloid adver-
tiser. "See who can find the cheapest room."

"And a job for me."

"When you're up to it. I can chance a job where I
don't come in contact with the public."

"Or need identification. A police check would be
interesting."

We read in silence for a minute. "Here's a job for
you," he said, smiling. "God, there must be thirty of
them. 'Girls wanted, no experience necessary. Escort
service. Twelve dollars per hour guaranteed.' Blow
jobs extra."

I laughed, a new sensation. "Come on."

"You think I'm kidding?" He showed me one ad
that asked for British, French, and Greek girls. "You

believe it's nationality they're talking about?"

I looked at the section. "You know, this is an idea. They must have clients who want older women."

He frowned at me. "You're not serious."

"I am indeed." I lowered my voice. "I don't mean *fucking* them. It's an escort service, after all. I get dolled up and let some poor old guy squire me around for a few hours, and when he pops the question, I say no. Hell, I can take care of myself."

He nodded slowly. "You know, you may be right. They certainly wouldn't expect you to work under your real name. Probably the best pay either of us could get, under the circumstances."

That was true, because "the circumstances," although I hadn't yet discussed this with him, included keeping Nick absolutely out of sight until he had his power back. Not even grocery shopping. Nick certainly had some idea of how thorough they could be in searching for someone. But *I* was the authority on what they could do if they found you.

Most of the men were likable enough, older fellows too shy or too busy to go through the slow excruciation of senior-citizen dating. A few had some unusual ideas about the way of a man with a maid, but it's hard to shock an abnormal-psychology professor, or even a normal one. About half of them really just wanted someone to talk to; someone who would listen respectfully. The half who wanted to get their rocks off were satisfied with quick masturbation, which I could do almost as dispassionately as a massage. I never mentioned that to Nick, though. He's more reasonable than most men, but he's still a man.

It only took two weeks to get a thousand dollars ahead. (All the income I've lost, teaching in college!) That was my arbitrary cut-off point. I bought a soldering gun and a sackful of components at Radio Shack and then picked up kits for wave generator, preamp, simple oscilloscope, and a small amplifier at a Heathkit shop. Then I got some aloe ointment at the drugstore, since I've never soldered for a day without being burned at least once, even without poor clumsy Nick as my helper/holder.

We did collect a few burns a day, but in one ninety-hour week we got everything assembled. Just in time. The rent was due, and I didn't want to go out manhandling for it.

Nick turned on the machine and asked me to stand on my head and whistle Dixie. I did a credible job, for a forty-five-year-old indoor woman who can't whistle (he mercifully cut me short after a couple of bars). We asked the landlord to come in, and he not only forgave us the rent but insisted on giving us twenty dollars for groceries. That was fun. Greasy slumlord.

But we did have a problem. The apparatus took up as much room as a large stereo component set. We couldn't really plug together a bunch of extension cords and haul it down to the sidewalk, so our victims were limited to people who could be enticed into our lair.

I have to admit that the first solution that occurred to me was a thoroughly immoral one. I could go back into the hand-job business and enveigle the customers up to our apartment. A lot of them were well-heeled family men who wouldn't miss a few hundred bucks, or at least wouldn't try to track it down. Instead, I came up with a technological "fix." Good old American know-how.

Sound waves can be reflected, refracted, and focused just like light waves. I remember how, in high school physics club, we made a "sound magnifier" out of a balloon filled with carbon dioxide. My approach would be a little different.

Various firms make "remote microphones," which are just plain microphones braced in front of a reflecting bowl. The bowl, which is a paraboloid, focuses onto the microphone all the sound waves that are coming from whatever direction you point it. They sell the things for bird-watching, supposedly. No harm done if a chatty neighbor gets in the way, right?

It occurred to me that you could reverse the thing —replace the microphone with a sound generator, and you would get the sonic equivalent of a searchlight! It could send a beam of ultrasonic whine for blocks, along with whispered commands.

I called up Edmund Scientific in New Jersey and had one of the things sent C.O.D. We scrounged another couple of hundred from the landlord to pay for it and keep us going in the meantime.

It came in three days and only took an hour to set up. It worked beautifully. Nick would sit down on the stoop, in view of our window, and wait until a prosperous-looking person came by. (In our neighborhood, that meant dope dealer or pimp.) Nick would ask him for a light, which would immobilize him long enough for me to line up the searchlight on him. Then Nick would ask whether the guy could spare a couple of bucks. If he reached for his wallet, we knew the machine was working, and we'd clean him out, erase the memory, and send him on his way.

On the third day, we stopped a handsome black dude who had a specially made thick wallet that produced seventeen thousand dollars in hundred-dollar bills. Nick asked whether he had any more money on

him, and from various pockets he produced five
shrink-wrapped packages of ten thousand dollars
each. We decided it might be healthy to move across
town that afternoon.

With over seventy-five grand to work with, we
could easily have hired out the job of miniaturizing
the signal generator and hiding it inside a watch. But
the person who made it might wonder about its function. So we had to be a little circumspect.

We found a small firm in Fort Lauderdale, Sun-
coast Micro-engineering, that would probably be able
to make the watch. I rigged up the searchlight device
to work with a cigarette-lighter rectifier, and we
rented a van without windows. Backed up to the
place so I could get a bead on the front door. Then
Nick went inside and engaged the president of the
firm with a line of convincing bullshit (was that a
talent he learned at KGB school? MIT?) and invited
him to lunch. They stepped out the door, and I snared
him; we found out from him who would be the best
technician for the job and then snared *him*. In ten
days, Nick was wearing a Svengali Timex on his
wrist.

All this time we'd been making plans—or rather,
Nick had been talking about the future, and I had
been listening. I guess I was waiting for him to come
up with something I could live with. But he never
did.

What Nick wanted was for both of us to undergo
radical plastic surgery—an unpleasant prospect, but
one that I agreed was probably necessary. We parted
company very profoundly on what to do after that,
though.

Nick wanted us to find a hidey-hole, some country
place or idyllic island, where we would go to ground

and hide for the rest of our lives. All right; I could see that eventually.

But first there were some things that had to be done.

CHAPTER TWENTY-FOUR

NICK

I TOLD VALERIE the truth about the two Bulgarians and the shootout with Tarakan, who I could almost honestly say was the first person I'd ever killed. I couldn't tell her about all the desperados I've talked into killing themselves, obviously—though in fact it hadn't occurred to me at the time to mention them; I don't think about them in that context.

The idea of the magic watch fascinated her. She'd had the process halfway figured out from what Shilkov had revealed with his questions, combined with her own memory of the pivotal undressing experiment. She didn't question my saying that I'd never used it for professional advancement, which was true, or for personal gain, except while I was "on the lam." I admitted having been tempted to turn the thing on to encourage sexual favors, but had so far resisted the temptation. I'm not sure she believed me about that, about resisting, but it didn't seem very important to her.

Our real falling out came over what to do with it *now*. I was ready to retire from the spy business, and you'd think she would be triply ready. But no; she wanted me to go out with a real bang.

Our new apartment, after I'd hit the dope dealer for $67,000, was a furnished penthouse in western Miami, nowhere near the ocean. From our twenty-fifth-floor balcony we had a fine view of a hundred square miles of urban sprawl and hot, low smog. It was on that balcony, while I was grilling shrimp and scallops *en brochette,* that she divulged her grandiose, if nonspecific, plans for my future. I had to admit that I didn't find the idea completely unattractive.

"We can't just use this thing to get a grubstake and go to some island to play Gauguin or Robert Louis Stevenson," she said.

"I'm not suggesting anything that bucolic," I said. "We can't afford to be conspicuous, wherever we go. Has to be a place with lots of Americans or Europeans."

"That's not what I mean. I mean we can't just use the watch to make money, get security, and then put it away in a safe deposit box. We should use it to *do* something!"

"I think I know what you're getting at." I turned the skewers and started brushing the seafood with lemon butter. "I wonder whether you've thought it through in as much detail as I have."

"Maybe not. But it seems to me you could get next to any politician, even the president of the United States, you know, put a bee in his bonnet. Cooperation with the Russians, world peace . . . something."

"Sure. And have you considered what would happen if I got caught? If any government got hold of this, even a so-called free one, it would destroy the social contract forever. No need for that government to give any rights to the governed—you just tell them to do what you want them to do. For their own good, of course." I picked at a scallop with a fork; not quite done yet. "In a matter of months, every government in the world knows the 'secret.' Can you imagine Stalin with a tool like that? Hitler? Make Genghis Khan look like a social worker."

"But you'd be okay as long as nobody tumbled to it. You've kept it secret this long."

"Because I've been able to stay in hiding; only come out on my own terms. How many layers of people do you think I'd have to bluff my way through to get to the president's ear? And how could I be sure I wasn't being recorded?"

"Of course you'd have to be careful."

"Careful as I was with that guy from Watergate? I got him killed because someone was listening."

She looked out over the city with her mouth set in a stubborn line. "Look," I continued, "they don't even have to get the watch. Don't have to know the frequency. If they just deduce the simple fact that there is a noise that will make people do what you say—"

"I know. They'll find out what the noise is."

"In no time. Especially since it's a pure tone. If it were a chord or a mixture of harmonics, or if it had to be a certain amplitude, it could take them forever. Trial and error. But hell. They could deduce that it was either ultrasonic or subsonic, and they'd just run up and down the scale. Probably find it in a couple of days' systematic searching."

"Yeah, maybe. I'm going to open that bottle of wine. Toss the salad." With a posture of resignation, perhaps calculated, she headed for the kitchen. This is the way she normally wins arguments with me. Halfway conceding that I'm right, and letting me talk myself over toward her position.

Of course I also had a certain amount of guilt pushing me into a desire to use this power for good, for a change. Not so much the trail of dead pushers, pimps, and muggers; that disturbed me, but more because I didn't understand it than out of feeling remorse for them. No, the main source of guilt was Valerie's suffering. I'd proceeded with such a slow pace supposedly to protect her—but had to come in with all the subtlety of a firestorm anyhow. I could have done that the first day I'd seen the message in the paper. I could have done it the night I came home from Paris.

Besides, I'd accepted a small risk of exposure every time I'd used the watch down in the Zone. What if some undercover cop had witnessed me asking a pimp to throw himself in front of a speeding bus? The power would have wound up in the hands of the authorities that way, just as surely as it would if they caught me whispering into the president's ear. And the payoff could be so much greater, the potential to change things . . .

Virtually the whole plan came to me in an instant. Valerie returned with the wine and salad, and we served each other in silence. Finally I spoke up.

"I've been thinking about what you said."

"So?"

"Leningrad is beautiful in the spring. We should go there."

CHAPTER TWENTY-FIVE

PRESIDENT NIXON MET the Russians in Moscow and President Ford met them in Vladivostok, and then for a long time the two countries' leaders stayed off each other's soil. They communicated by diplomatic pouch and phone in the best of times, and in the worst, only through inflammatory rhetoric in *Pravda* and the *New York Times*.

President Gideon Fitzpatrick wanted to change that. A neoconservative with impeccable anti-Communist credentials, he was safe including in his platform a proposal to get together with the Russians and "try to talk some sense into them." Their meeting would be more symbolic than substantial, but it would open a new round of formal talks on arms limitation, cultural and scientific exchange, and the possibility of restoring to the Soviet Union "most favored nation" import-export status—which not incidentally would put the fear of God, or at least the Almighty Dollar, into the Chinese and Japanese.

President Fitzpatrick did have one important emotional tie with Russia and, not too indirectly, with the new Soviet premier. On 25 April 1945, as a very young and green lieutenant in the 69th Infantry Division, he waded ashore on the eastern bank of the Elbe, to be greeted by cheers and incomprehensible gibberish and a canteen cup full of vodka. By dawn he could almost understand Russian. At least he could sing the first few bars of the Soviet national anthem.

He was not so happy with the Russians in subsequent years and decades, though not even the McCarthy era could permanently affect his preference for vodka. (A very junior senator at the time, in public he did drink bourbon for a couple of years.)

Premier Sergei Vardanyan was also a soldier in the Great Patriotic War, a private even younger than Fitzpatrick, and they may possibly have come in sight of one another that April. Vardanyan's unit arrived at the Elbe the day before Fitzpatrick's moved on, and they were stationed barely ten miles apart.

The plan was for them to meet again at the Elbe (now part of East Germany), on the anniversary of the historic occasion, and deliver speeches and lay wreaths. Then Fitzpatrick would make *pro forma* visits to various European allies, leading up to his meeting with Vardanyan on April 30. The next day, he would be the first American president to observe May Day on Soviet soil.

To be fair to his predecessors, most American presidents since 1918 couldn't have stood in that reviewing stand—not with a bellicose procession of tanks and guns and missiles rolling by. But since Brezhnev's time, May Day has been quite the opposite, a gentle celebration of peace. Every factory and school has a float done up with doves and rosy-cheeked girls, papier-mâché globes; all presided over by the benevolent hammer and sickle and the word for peace: *mir*. (Nowadays the guns don't go on parade until they celebrate the October Revolution, in November.)

The special assistants and secretariats in charge of
protocol did a certain amount of horse trading prior to
the announcement of the event. The premier and the
president would stand together not in Moscow, where
the rest of the Presidium, Supreme Soviet, Council of
Ministers, Party bigwigs, and other *apparatchiki*
would be. Fitzpatrick held out for Leningrad, within
breathing distance of non—Warsaw Pact Europe. The
Russian protocol people let it be, rather than queer
the deal.

Fitzpatrick was also allowed to bring into the country a planeload of people and things that would not
have to submit to the indignity of inspection: his family; a cook with a kitchen and a week's supply of
bland, safe food; a veritable gaggle of discreetly but
heavily armed Secret Service men and women; and a
handful of Soviet specialists and translators.

Chief among the translators, if things worked out
right, would be the most dangerous man in the world.

CHAPTER TWENTY-SIX

JACOB

FOUR SOVIET SPIES found dead, and blood from a fifth person, in a factory building not ten miles from Langley. Nothing about it was made public—the FBI leaned on the press like a huge unfriendly planet—but the next day the Soviet embassy was demanding an explanation, privately but very strongly. There was precedent for a revenge motive, harking back to the Reagan years, if you believe rumors. They murdered one of our spies in cold blood, and we retaliated by killing ten of theirs the next day, in various places around Europe.

But we didn't do this. Two of the male spies were killed by the same weapon, a .45 automatic, with two accurately placed shots apiece. The other two, a man and a woman, were executed grotesquely, handcuffed together around a chair leg. The woman's abdomen was slashed open, from the navel down, with a razor —or scalpel. The man was castrated. Whoever did it had evidently watched their struggles for several minutes and then finished them off by severing the carotid arteries. There's nothing like that in any CIA handbook I'm familiar with.

Jefferson and I, because of our direct involvement

with the Scalpel's current activities, had to fly down to Washington and stay up all night with a couple of Soviet Affairs people and an espionage woman from the FBI, cobbling together a report for the Soviet embassy. About half truth and half invention, it certainly didn't tell them anything the KGB didn't already know, but it did squarely place the blame for the multiple murder on Mikhail Shilkov, a.k.a. the Scalpel. We included a blood-chemistry workup from the fifth person, assuming he was the murderer, suggesting that they compare it with KGB records. It could have been from a fifth victim, though, spirited away for some reason. Like Valerie Foley. (The next afternoon it occurred to me to ask the FBI whether she could have been the victim. They said the sample contained so much testosterone that if it belonged to a woman, she'd shave her face twice a day and sing bass.)

We don't have a mole deep enough in the KGB to know exactly what the result was—or perhaps we do, and I don't have the "need to know"—but an East German KGB man who also works for us relayed an order from Moscow that Shilkov, whose whereabouts were unknown, was to be retained for questioning if he showed up, with force if necessary; killed if necessary.

Circumstantial evidence, but good enough for us. The FBI sent out a mailing to every hospital in the country, with a picture of the Scalpel. Did anyone like this show up on February 19 or soon after, seeking treatment for a serious wound? He'd lost more than a quart of blood.

We did get a positive identification, but by then the trail was cold. A couple of weeks later, a country doctor in Unionville, Maryland, saw the picture on a hospital visit and said sure, he'd treated the guy. The wound was badly infected and had been sutured by an amateur—Shilkov claimed that it had happened during a deep-woods camping expedition; he'd done the stitchery himself. The doctor drained and dressed the wound and wrote a prescription for antibiotics, and gently gave him a psychiatric referral. Then it was ten days before he dropped by the Frederick hospital and saw the picture.

So Shilkov could be anywhere by now, and Foley could be anywhere, and we never have had the faintest idea where Mrs. Foley was. Did they all come together in Cabin John on February 19?

Jefferson pointed out a grisly possibility. The couple who were so characteristically slashed apart may not have been killed by Shilkov, but by someone who wanted to implicate him. The other two could have been killed by anyone who was an accurate pistol shot—such as Nicholas Foley.

Or maybe it was a matter unrelated to the Foley case. A specialist like Shilkov could have come to the United States on multiple assignments. Like the Boston murder, the bloodbath could have been an internal KGB affair, an interrogation that got out of hand. Though in that case you wouldn't expect the Soviet embassy to press for an explanation. Unless they were trying to misdirect us.

Jefferson and I got to the Cabin John scene after midnight. There was still a POLICE LINE—DO NOT CROSS cordon around the building, but only a couple of freezing rookies guarding things. The FBI espionage specialist had come along with us.

They'd taken the bodies away, leaving only improbably large frozen splashes of clotted blood and stacks of Polaroid color glossies showing the disposition of the corpses at the time of discovery. The FBI woman made it as far as the pictures of the mutilated bodies and then ran outside to throw up. I felt like following her. Jefferson didn't look too good, either.

The man at the center of all this is a self-effacing, witty fellow who was the most popular teacher in his department, a family man with impeccable academic, military, and professional credentials. Is it always this way? They interview the neighbors of a mass murderer and he was invariably a nice guy who loved children and took care of his aged parents. He never pulls the wings off flies or brags about his collection of snuff movies.

The expression on the face of the castrated man will stay with me forever. I'll be eligible for retirement in two years. Will I last that long?

CHAPTER TWENTY-SEVEN

NICK

WE DECIDED TO drive when we left Miami, rather than push our luck with airports. Somewhere in Washington or Boston there might be a picture of James Norwood, not resembling Robert Redford. And of course they had pictures of Valerie.

Valerie pointed out that a "style" disguise would be more effective than any false-wig kind of masquerade. So although it hurt, we each bought a complete tacky-polyester wardrobe from K-Mart, got absurd haircuts, and made the trip to Mexico in a bright-yellow Mercury station wagon, five years old, with HONK IF YOU LOVE JESUS stickered on the bumper. Nearly two hundred people loved Jesus between Miami and Zacatecas. We waved and smiled and honked back.

We were going to Mexico to get new faces. What I'd done, in the course of one night, was work my way up the Miami dope-dealing ladder, starting with a smooth-talking cocaine retailer in a notorious disco in Coconut Grove and winding up in the company of a dark man dressed all in silk, in the Cuban quarter, who dealt only in tens of kilograms. His English was no better than my Spanish, but between the two he understood and answered my question: Where would one go to have a new face constructed surgically and be certain the law wouldn't know? He told me about the Clínico Libre de Zacatecas—the "free clinic" of Zacatecas—and generously gave me an attaché case full of hundred-dollar bills, because the name was a sarcasm. For some reason I let him live, and all the others who led me to him. Maybe I'm getting soft, and sane. Maybe I just know that when one dies, another has replaced him within an hour. Like malignant cells, or the brooms in *The Sorcerer's Apprentice*. Our humanly bottomless capacity for evil. As if I were in a position to pass judgment.

The four-day drive from Miami to the border was pleasant, cruising along the Gulf Coast highway, putting on our lower-middle-class hick act whenever we got out of the car. We were able to keep straight faces most of the time, though I lost it once in a San Antonio souvenir shop, when Valerie bought a pair of sunglasses that looked like a prop from an old Buck Rogers movie. Even the clerk who rang them up was trembling with suppressed laughter.

We crossed the border at Nuevo Laredo after midnight, as I had been advised to do, and palmed the Customs guard a twenty-dollar bill, being deliberately clumsy and obvious. He chalked Xs on all our luggage, letting us pass without opening any of them. On the other side of the border we rested at a Mexican Holiday Inn, where the night clerk converted three of our hundred-dollar bills into pesos, at a creative rate of exchange. We started south at first light.

The road to Zacatecas had some roller-coaster twists and turns in the mountains, but was mostly a ruler-straight line through dusty desert, with occasional small, dusty towns, and the larger cities Monterrey and Saltillo, also dusty. Actually, we both would have liked to slow down and see the country, which had a spare beauty neither of us had experienced before, but there were time constraints. Radical plastic surgery isn't an outpatient procedure, and they weren't going to delay the summit while I healed.

We spent the night in the suburbs of Saltillo, again leaving at first light, and arrived in Zacatecas in the early afternoon. First we went to a bank and rented the largest safe-deposit box we could buy, filling it completely with hundred-dollar bills. That left us with three packets of ten thousand dollars each, for spending money.

The Free Clinic didn't advertise in the streets, didn't have an address in any directory. We'd been told to look up one Eduardo de Rivera at 26 Hidalgo. Of course he wasn't in, and the housekeeper didn't know where we could find him or when he'd be back. We sat in an outdoor cantina on the other side of the street for a couple of hours watching the door. When a man in a business suit rushed up to it, we were right behind him. Cutting short our introductions, he ushered us in hurriedly and turned us over to the housekeeper, saying he'd be back in a few minutes, and ran upstairs.

Like all the other residences on the block, 26 Hidalgo looked rundown from the outside, just a crumbling dusty adobe wall with a heavy door, double-locked and braced with metal bands. Inside, the place was opulent. Thick carpets and expensive woods in large, cool rooms with high ceilings, brass fixtures gleaming labor-intensively. Medieval wall hangings and pre-Columbian sculptures. We passed a grand piano and an ornately carved antique billiard table on our way to the atrium, where the housekeeper, Consuelo, seated us in comfortable wicker chairs in front of a trickling fountain that was very old and ostentatiously Italian. There was a riot of orchids in planters around the room, and exotic dwarf fruit trees. Wordlessly, she brought a bottle of Dom Pérignon and three crystal fluted glasses. She poured two of them and disappeared.

Valerie toasted me. "I think we've been in the wrong racket all these years."

"Doing all right now, though." I switched to Larry Martino's soft, refined voice. "Here he comes."

Señor de Rivera had traded his coat and tie for a cardigan pullover. He looked like Carl Sagan back in the seventies. The man who came down with him looked like George Raft in the thirties. Silent, unsmiling, stuffed into a dark suit. He obviously had company in the suit, .45 caliber or so. He stayed at the entrance to the atrium, unfortunately out of the watch's range.

De Rivera's English had an unexpected Hebrew accent. I later learned he had grown up in Argentina at a time when being Jewish was becoming more and more dangerous, and so had gone to college and medical school in Tel Aviv, where he first learned the tongue of Shakespeare and Henny Youngman. "It is a face-lift you want," he said. "One or both?"

"Both of us want some modification," I said. "For me, a combination: rhytidectomy, rhinoplasty, mentoplasty, and blepharoplasty. . . ."

"Okay." He put a finger to his lips. "You have looked into it. Face-lift, nose reconstruction, chin augmentation, eye-lift. Expensive and painful. You are sure, or you want advice?"

"I'll take advice."

"Okay. You aren't doing this so you look pretty. You're doing this so that someone looks at you, he sees someone else."

"That's right."

"Okay. I can make you look young like your own son. Brow-lift and then hair transplant to cover the scars."

"I'd like that, but the hair transplant takes months, doesn't it?" He nodded. "I have to be out of here in five or six weeks."

"Okay. The other procedures should be do-able in that time. The swelling will be down by then, and the scars not too obvious. Perhaps some numbness. Even paralysis. You are not young." He turned to Valerie. "Señora. You also must leave in six weeks?"

"Maybe five," she said.

"Okay. Face-lift, eye-lift, brow-lift. I would say. Then hair dye and careful practice with makeup, new patterns. Forgive me, but you are not used to makeup."

"I don't normally wear any. It's part of this disguise."

"Sure, okay. We have a woman here who can teach you everything." He reached under the cardigan and brought out a calculator, which he held up to the light for a few seconds, then started punching: "Two face-lifts ... two eye-lifts. One of each ... brow-lift, rhinoplasty, mentoplasty. Look," he said, pointing at me, "I can make your ears not stick out so much, too. But you got to wear a band around your head while you sleep, maybe six weeks."

"I'd better not chance it."

"Okay. American dollars?" I said yes. "That will be two hundred fourteen thousand dollars, cash in advance."

"Ouch. That's almost ten times as much as the States."

"Okay, so go to the Mayo Clinic. Maybe they take Medicare for it, hm? Maybe State Farm?"

"I'll tell you what. We won't haggle over the price.

You'll get your two hundred grand. But we give you half when you begin the procedures and the other half when we're satisfied with the results."

He slowly replaced the calculator, staring at nothing. "Look. Number one, I should do it over and over until you like your looks? What do you mean 'satisfied'?"

"Just that we look radically different."

"Okay, that much I can always guarantee. But like I say, there might be some paralysis. Maybe some pain we have to go in after at some later date."

"That's all right."

"Okay, number two. I got to have cash in advance because there are so many people involved. I just do the rhytidectomies. I got to fly in people from all over the place for the other procedures. A hundred thousand won't do it."

"Oh, baloney," Valerie said. "You fly in four people to do our eyes and noses. That's eight thousand dollars first-class airfare, max, if they all live in Tasmania. Leaves enough to pay them each more than twenty thousand dollars for a day's work. If they get more than that, I'm gonna walk out of here and go to medical school."

He looked hurt. "There are more than four people."

"The offer stands," I said, and turned on the watch, unnecessarily.

He stared away for a few seconds and then nodded. "Okay, you bring me the hundred and seven and we'll start calling people."

I took the three packages of bills out of my pockets, and Valerie opened her purse. "Would you pick up the phone for sixty?"

He slit the plastic of one with a thumbnail and pulled a bill out of the middle. He held it up to the light and studied it closely, then crumpled it up and smoothed it out. "Okay. Forgive me, but I had a patient once who printed his own money."

"A reasonable precaution. We have a precaution, too: We don't both go under at the same time. One of us must always be awake while the other's in surgery."

He stacked up the six packets. "Actually, that's not an unusual arrangement. Sometimes they even want an observer in the operating room. That's awkward. Federico"—he looked up at the George Raft character—"*Telefonea un taxi para los estimados señores.*"

He stood up and bowed slightly. "Federico will tell you when your taxi comes. Be here tomorrow at nine o'clock . . . and, Señora, don't eat any breakfast. We'll work on you first."

"This is the clinic, here?" she asked.

He smiled. "Indeed. The smallest and most expensive hospital in Mexico."

CHAPTER TWENTY-EIGHT

VALERIE

NICK SAID IT feels like having been on the losing end of a fistfight, this long healing period. I wouldn't know. I was glad for the strong painkillers.

For weeks we were virtual prisoners at 26 Hidalgo, claustrated in a set of rooms that had no mirrors. Of course we could see each other, and lied about what we saw.

It was doubly painful, watching Nick agonize through the surgical procedures and also watching his face disappear, the man I've loved for more than half my life. I think of myself as practical rather than romantic. But no one is completely one or the other, I guess.

His chin augmentation gave me the shudders. They make a long incision in the gum, between front teeth and lower lip, and slide a piece of plastic down over your chinbone. It gave him a Kirk Douglas profile. I'd just started getting used to his chin, after all these years of seeing hair. Now I have twice as much chin to get used to.

Both of us temporarily got bright-red bloody sclera (the "whites" of the eyes) from the eye-lifts, and since Nick couldn't wear contacts after the operation, they brought him a pair of eyeglasses. I could see my vague reflection in them, enough to tell that Zacatecas was better off not having me on the streets for a while.

I was just as glad not to have the rhinoplasty, which gave Nick hell for almost a week, cotton packing jammed up his nose, an itchy cast taped over half his face. My brow-lift was a lot easier, though for a couple of weeks afterward I felt like I was doomed to walk around for the rest of my life with an expression of perpetual wide-eyed amazement.

There was no magical transition scene like you see in the movies, the surgeon slowly unwrapping the coils of bandage to reveal Natalie Wood bathed in soft light, radiant, impeccably coiffed. Instead, the bruises went from purple to blue to brown to green to yellow, and disappeared; meanwhile, the stitches came out, one set after another. Then one day we looked just like normal people, if strangers and a little under the weather.

They dyed my hair coal black and showed me how to use makeup dramatically, Latin style. Nick kept his ash-blond bleach job but started to brush his hair straight back, rather than part it. He looked like a man about forty, prematurely balding. I looked younger. De Rivera offered to complete the job with a thirty-five-thousand-dollar breast-and-ass lift, but I said no, *gracias*. I didn't plan to go back into the escort business. Besides, whatever this figure's shortcomings, I have worked hard for its virtues.

We walked around Zacatecas for a few days, getting a feel for freedom after so many weeks of confinement in our elegant prison, our stifling bandages. It's a good town for exercise, very up and down. A couple of the sidewalks are so steep they had steps molded into them.

We also practiced being our new selves. The Free Clinic documents your new identity pretty thoroughly. Nick was Anson Rafferty, an unemployed-by-choice linguistics professor who lives in Miami with me, his wife, Linda, woman of some means. "Rafferty" was a person Nick had made up while he was working for the CIA: a man who spoke fluent Russian and had done some contract work for the Agency in the sixties and seventies.

We had a family passport with four years' worth of travel in Europe and South America; we made up and memorized consistent stories about the places we'd been, which was sort of fun. Florida driver's licenses and an assortment of credit cards—the American Express Gold Card being in my name, naturally. We had a post office box in Miami where birth and marriage certificates were waiting (since it would seem suspicious to be carrying those around). They even went so far as to supply us with an assortment of appropriate business cards and receipts. Nick says they call that "pocket litter" in the spy biz.

I would have liked to relax in Zacatecas for a long time. Clean mountain air, cool mornings, warm afternoons. No KGB agents but my husband, and I didn't mind him spying on me. But we had to get back to the muggy traffic clot of Miami and get to work. Since it was my idea, at least nominally, I couldn't object.

We left the polyester disguises and Mercury station wagon for the clinic to hock and took an asthmatic puddle jumper to Guadalajara, where I put together a wardrobe for us from boutiques and a classy used-clothing store. Opened an obscenely large dollar account at the largest bank, with cash, and then closed it with a check. They didn't even blink. Then we caught a comfy 777 back to Miami, where Customs scrutinized us for a half hour and found nothing. If they'd come upon the $397,850 cashier's check, it might have given them pause, but it wasn't illegal. The only illegal things we were smuggling in were sealed behind new faces.

We still had the lease on the West Miami high rise, but didn't go back, in case they had trailed us that far—the CIA, the KGB, or the people who'd given us the attaché case full of money. We picked up the documents claiming we had been born and married, and drove a rented car north until we got tired, West Palm Beach. I opened an account with the cashier's check and got a fancy television set as a premium. (I could have chosen a grandfather clock instead, but decided it would look tacky in the hotel room.) Then I wrote checks to three other banks, opening CD accounts in my name and a smallish joint checking account in one, just thirty grand.

We slept twelve hours, and then Nick started the delicate business of getting a job as President Fitzpatrick's Russian translator. He had put the wheels in motion before we left for Mexico.

We'd found out that Fitzpatrick's usual translator, in French as well as in Russian, was J. Cameron Lambert, a general in the Air Force Reserve and dedicated party hack. He had done a lot of work in the primaries and delivered at least New Hampshire, and this was his reward: Special Assistant to the President for Intergovernmental Affairs and Assistant Director of Presidential Foreign Advance. He was a robust man in his midsixties, who was about to fall ill with the flu. Unable to make the Russian trip, he would recommend his old friend Anson Rafferty. Speaks Russkie like a native. Real patriot. Did some hush-hush work for the CIA, never could tell me what it was about. President Fitzpatrick would be a sucker for that; he loved spy stuff.

When Nick had created the dossier on Rafferty, he'd put his own fingerprints in the file, but the picture was his old new face, and he'd only given a sketchy background. So before he made the move on J. Cameron Lambert, he had to make sure that Anson Rafferty existed as a whole paper person, with an up-to-date photograph. That meant he had to talk his way into the right file room at Langley. He made some phone calls.

To give us a West Palm address, I rented a swank efficiency under my mother's maiden name. Then I went to the bank to get us traveling money and ran into an annoying wall of tellers and vice-presidents: "You can't draw on this account; your check hasn't cleared." But it was a cashier's check. "We have no record of what kind of check it was: there will be a ten- to fourteen-day waiting period." Let me get my husband.

Nick came in with his watch and withdrew twenty thousand in small bills from the account of a real estate firm with its main office in Bogotá. He conducted the transaction from a vice-president's office, so that his face wouldn't be on the teller's camera.

Packing for the trip, I had to admit I was getting to like this strange life. Not many people have to leave clothes behind because there's too much money clogging the suitcase.

We took the first morning flight to Washington and set up shop. Nick had me do the detail work while he went out to keep a couple of appointments at Langley. "Anson Rafferty" had a post office box in Georgetown, which was a solid jam of advertising circulars. I rented us an apartment only a couple of blocks from Nick's old one. We had to assume that the "James

Norwood" identity was no longer safe, though Nick
had set up a cover story about a year's sabbatical.
People might wonder why he didn't look like Robert
Redford anymore.

The second day Nick came home tired but in a
good humor. He opened a bottle of beer and sat down
in front of the picture window that looked out on the
quiet street. Six weeks had made a big difference in
Washington; instead of snow, buds and even blooms.
Downtown the cherry blossoms were riotously declaring Japanese-American solidarity. Our street had
dogwood, for resurrection and hope. I got a glass and
sat down next to him and helped him with his beer.

"I really think it's going to work," he said. "I
really do."

"Did you get to the translator today?"

"Lambert, yeah. No problem. He keeps an office
next to Blair House; I just talked my way past a couple of secretaries and invited him to lunch. Walked a
few blocks to the Hofbrau. I finished most of the
convincing before we got to the restaurant.

"Turns out he wasn't enthusiastic about going to
Leningrad anyway. He's been there twice before, and
both times his arthritis gave him hell for months."

"The water?"

"Foreigners don't drink the water. Not even people
from Moscow. You can preserve small animals in it.
He thinks it was something in the air.

"Anyhow, I told him he was going to start coming
down with the flu this afternoon. He's to call Fitzpatrick and beg off, suggesting me as a substitute. I
don't suppose the president has called."

"No . . . I'm almost sure I would've remembered."

"Right." He ruffled my hair. "Lambert would normally go out a week or ten days ahead of time, with

the advance protocol team. I'll do that too, but we'll have one of Lambert's assistants to do the actual time juggling and fork counting. I just want to meet the Soviet translators and, if possible, the premier. Make sure the machine works on everybody."

"What if the premier's hard of hearing? He's pretty old."

"Nothing in his CIA file about it. Lots about his digestion and back problems. No way to tell, of course, except try the machine. Same with Fitzpatrick. He's older."

We both jumped when the phone rang. It was the president's social secretary, asking whether Mr. Rafferty would like to join Mr. and Mrs. Fitzpatrick for lunch tomorrow. Nick got me included in the invitation.

We split another beer over that, and I got so nervous, I had to go out and buy a new dress, cursing myself for personifying a cartoon cliché female. It was a nice dress, though, and the shoes and purse and hat weren't bad either.

We'd been told apologetically to arrive at least a half hour early, to accommodate security requirements. The Secret Service men and women were thorough, and not remarkably polite about it. It's a good thing Nick had found my FBI file and fiddled with the fingerprint record. Aging Radical Apprehended Sneaking Into White House Luncheon.

The social secretary eventually rescued us from the minions of the law and ushered us down to the Rose Room, where we were seated at a four-person table and plied with California wine, politically correct but unexciting. After about ten minutes, the president and Mrs. Fitzpatrick came bustling down. He declined the vin du Ernest and Julio in favor of a symbolic martini with more olive than vodka.

It's hard not to be in awe of a president, even if you voted against him. The White House sings with power, the continuity of power, and the tenant may be temporary, but he's the focus of it all. Fitzpatrick didn't just bask in it. He glowed.

I found myself wondering what he'd been like before—how much of his undeniable charm and charisma was the power of high office amplified through an appropriate, perhaps carefully invented, persona. Whether he'd be as impressive as a college dean or a shopkeeper. Well, he hadn't been chosen at random. There had to be a lot of mana there from the beginning.

I'd never had pheasant under glass before. I could make it a habit.

Molly Fitzpatrick and I mostly ate and listened while our husbands exchanged observations and ideas about the Russians and the upcoming trip. Nick seemed convincing in his worldly, conservative Rafferty disguise. The two times he'd visited the Soviet Union before had been deep-cover CIA assignments around Kiev; Fitzpatrick had been briefed about them. (If he knew that all of Rafferty's putative supervisors for these assignments were now conveniently dead, he didn't mention it.) He assured us that even if the Soviets knew that Rafferty had done some work for the CIA, they wouldn't make an issue of it, so long as he wasn't actively spying anymore. They assume that any American who speaks Russian is a spook, anyhow.

The president took Nick upstairs to look at some of the classified arrangements, leaving his wife in charge of me. That got a little dicey.

Molly Fitzpatrick could have been a liability to a

politician with presidential ambitions. When they'd married, he was a recently widowed fifty-year-old; she was a girl barely twenty, a friend of the family who had helped look after their children. Twenty years later, she turned out to be a real asset, a symbol of Fitzpatrick's agelessness and his link to the young conservatives in both parties. Molly was the first actually glamorous woman to hold the "office" since Jacqueline Kennedy. She had only had a high school education, but she was as sharp as she was beautiful.

We were walking around the room with our sherry, looking at the paintings, when she dropped her bomb: "So how long has it been since the face-lift?"

I spilled a little wine. "Pardon?"

"Guess I'm too California. Forget it."

"No, really, I—I'm just surprised. I didn't think it showed."

"Takes one to know one. I got overhauled right after Gid got elected, wanted to be okay before the Inauguration. You think that wasn't a bitch. The reporters agreed not to notice, but for a while there I spent more time at the makeup table than an actress. You know, slowly *evolv*ing my new look. Even though I spent a month under wraps at the clinic, in Mexico."

Good God. "Zacatecas?" I regretted it the moment I said it.

"Take what?"

"Oh, that's the town where my clinic was. Where in Mexico?"

"Yeah, I was down in Acapulco. Didn't get much sun an' fun, though. Sort of sit around and try not to pick at the stitches."

"I know, they start itching the day they stop hurting."

"It was nice, though; I'll give you the name of the

place. I'm goin' down every eight or ten years until, you know, it doesn't make any difference. Every room has its own swimming pool out front and every morning somebody throws a handful of rose petals on the water."

"I could live with that."

"Yeah. So how come you got it? I mean, not to criticize, God knows, but for me it was kind of a cold-blooded thing, professional thing; for eight more years I've gotta be Gid's little girl. It wasn't out of vanity. You don't strike me as vain, either."

"Well . . ."

"Look, I know I'm way out of line. Like Gid says, I've got a real nose problem. Forget it."

"No, that's okay. With me I guess it was simple depression, the usual, a kind of therapy. Twenty-five years married, you know. Sort of dreading meno-pause and being an old lady."

She put a hand on my shoulder. "God, don't I know. Don't I know." We stopped at a painting of Martha Washington, looking prim and spinsterish. "You got to wonder. It must've been easier on them, none of this youth culture BS, no Hollywood, no *image* problems. 'Hey, I'm an old lady. That's what happens if you live long enough.' My grandmother, she lived in her eighties, and just seemed to love it. Putting up jam, you know, baby-sitting for every-body. I can't see myself that way. I'd even *like* to, but I can't." She laughed harshly. "I'm a rock-an'-*roll*er, for Christ sake. I can't be a *grand*mother!"

I had to laugh, too. I liked her. "Me, too. When I read that Ringo Starr was going bald, God, it put a chill down my spine."

"Yeah, and Gid would say 'Ringo Who?' Anson's a lot younger than that, isn't he?"

"Oh yeah." I felt a little twinge of Nick's kneejerk

paranoia. "A bit younger. Gid fought in World War Two?"

"That's right."

"I guess that makes him ten, fifteen years older." I took a chance, anticipating the next question. "Yeah, Anson went along with me to the clinic. Had a couple of tucks taken, I think mostly to make me feel better. He didn't want to get rid of the wrinkles, though, on his forehead. That would really take some years off him."

She sighed. "Gid won't even joke about it. He likes being an elder statesman."

"I think Anson feels some of that. Wrinkles are badges for men. They earn them; we just *get* them."

"Right." She started to say something but just shook her head.

Nick appeared, with the social secretary close behind. "We better get home and start packing," he said. "Headed for Helsinki tomorrow." We said goodbye to Molly and declined the Secret Service limousine. It was only a forty-five-minute walk, and we needed the exercise.

As prearranged, our conversation on the way home was "safe." The Secret Service had had our coats for three hours.

.

CHAPTER TWENTY-NINE

NICK

WE RESTED FOR a day and a half in Helsinki, catching up on eight time zones. I was surprised at how much Finnish I could understand. It had been half a century since my father spent the summer drilling it into me. Of course my current persona couldn't speak it, so I was carefully ignorant. I couldn't even tell Valerie when a schoolboy taunted the "old baldie with his arm around the young woman."

Some of the protocol party lived it up pretty desperately in Helsinki. It's a bustling modern city with a night life that goes on till dawn. The night life of Leningrad, they knew, would peter out about an hour after dinner. And it wasn't exactly casinos and raw sex. Maybe a crowded auditorium with folk dancing or ballet. More my speed, actually.

Valerie went along with the gang seeking fleshpots; I decided to stay at the hotel and relax in the sauna. But the sauna was not just a hot room and it was not particularly relaxing. An old lady with the strength of ten beat the hell out of my naked carcass and then alternately scalded and froze it. Afterward I felt like a cheap cut of meat that had been tenderized. Clean, though.

Thought I'd kill some time at the hotel casino, but I was too thoroughly knocked out. I'd barely had time to lose ten markkaa when I started to fall face forward into my Scotch. It was probably for the best. I slept the clock around and woke up feeling almost human. Valerie woke up about the same time, but creeped around like a wounded invertebrate, having bar-hopped, jet-lagging, till after two. I told her it was the bad example of Molly Fitzpatrick, born-again sex kitten, and she tried to make a face.

I'm more afraid of the First Lady than the CIA, especially from what Valerie said. She's a lovely and singular woman, but I think that if she gets curious about something, she will run it down like a hungry hound after a fox.

Could I kill her if it came to that? The stakes are sufficiently high to justify any person's death. I've never killed a woman.

The revelry continued aboard the Finnair flight to Leningrad, a lot of people dosing their hangovers with morning beers and caraway-flavored spirits. I had some cool tea and smoked reindeer, which made me feel vaguely guilty, like eating Donner or Blitzen or Rudolph the Red-nosed. Some KGB agent.

Leningrad was hidden under clouds. I was sorry for that; I'd looked forward to tracing out the districts of my old hometown from the air, finding the streets where I'd lived. So much was destroyed during the Siege, of course, and rebuilt. I'd read that the rebuilders had tried to be faithful to the original designs, even to details of finish, in many buildings.

That was good. I wanted to find my father's house. I wanted to see the one across the street, where I'd spent half my childhood playing. Until the war's fist flattened it. Until I saw Alex cough blood and die in his father's arms.

That's like another world, like a documentary movie I saw and remember well only in fragments. But in a curious way it's also like yesterday. With my eyes closed I can smell the dust and smoke, the cordite from the bombs; I can hear the thin screams of people buried in rubble, the neighbors shouting back as they claw through the debris, bombs and shells still falling, finally to pull out bloodied corpses grimy with the dust of pulverized brick and stone. The dead looked so calm. Beyond all of it, we say conventionally. But of course they are the most lasting part of it, really, until the memories of the last one of us who saw them also finally surrender to death.

Moscow gave our city a medal, the Order of Lenin. I remember my foster father suggesting that they beat it into a million pieces, one for each of the dead. He had made the calculation and showed me how large each splinter would be. A microscopic sliver for each of a million graves.

I came back from Rivertown for one day before flying to Canada and this odd life. My foster father was dead and my foster mother was in a hospital, too far buried in age and grief to recognize me. I took a bus out to the mass cemetery where most of the million are buried, and spent the afternoon there, pacing the fields of unmarked graves, vowing through youthful tears that this would not happen again, not to Mother Russia, not to anyone. We are vilified as sneaks and traitors and worse, we spies, but this is the truth: We normally win and lose our wars with no one dying. That's a large thing if you've lived through the usual kind of war.

Our diplomatic status should have allowed us to bypass Customs, but the KGB man in charge insisted that our papers were not in order. A pity the KGB doesn't have a secret handshake; perhaps I could have saved us some time and frustration.

They wanted to separate the three of us who knew some Russian from the nonspeakers, but that didn't work because Valerie and I were on the same passport. After twenty minutes of baleful stares and whispered conference, they evidently decided to treat us normally, i.e., alternating belligerent harassment with stony silence.

There are three kinds of KGB people prevalent in Russia. These flunkies were the border guards who keep the teeming hordes of aliens outside from rushing into the Soviet Union; they wore plain army uniforms with KGB insignia. The second type, the ones who keep an eye on Soviet citizens at home, also wear a sort of uniform, at least in the cities: rumpled dark suit, narrow tie, supercilious expression. Children may be afraid of them, but most Soviet citizens have learned to live with them, like living with mosquitoes or shortages. The third type is dangerous, because you may know one who looks and acts like anybody, and you think he works for the roads commission or the copyright office—until one day you learn that he was otherwise, and you should have been more careful about what you said between the eighth vodka and passing out.

(We—perhaps I should not say *we*—Americans who wax righteously horrified over this sort of thing might try to cast a clear eye on our own police state. It's true that most people go through life without knowingly running into a CIA or FBI agent. But our everyday police have guns, which is not the case in Russia, and some of them have too much of an itch about the trigger finger. And the liberties the Bill of Rights guarantees to us may not be available to Russians, but on the other hand, those rights are also routinely violated by the CIA and the FBI when an American citizen is presumed guilty. Anyone who thinks otherwise has his head in the sand.)

I held off using the watch because of the certainty that we were being examined and recorded. Finally I turned it on while a nineteen-year-old private was slowly, insolently, fingering his way through our luggage. I had to go to the bathroom.

"—Comrade," I said, carefully, "—we are not simple tourists, you know. You must speed up this process. If we are unnecessarily delayed, it could be hard on you."

He looked at me as if he were seeing me for the first time. "—Yes, Comrade. Of course." He gave the rest of the bags a cursory jostle and zipped them up.

Waiting for us on the other side were a brace of KGB men in the "civilian" uniform—rumpled dark suit—and a smiling fat man dressed in up-to-date Western business clothes.

"—Welcome to Russia, Dr. Rafferty," he said, shaking hands. "—I am Anatoly Menenkov, your opposite number. Premier Dr. Vardanyan's translator." He took Valerie's hand, bowed exactly forty-five degrees over it, and switched to English, a bland North Atlantic accent. "Mrs. Rafferty, a pleasure." He told her who he was. "My extrasensory perception tells me that you do not speak Russian."

"I'm afraid that's true."

"Oh, don't be apologetic." Menenkov gestured to the KGB men, and they picked up our luggage. "It puts me ahead of Dr. Rafferty. That much more practice."

Menenkov's car was a dark-red Mercedes, at least ten years old but scrupulously maintained, gleaming with many coats of lacquer. The KGB men put our luggage in the trunk, and one of them slid into the front seat while the other ordered us to wait here while he got the other car. Menenkov took the wheel, and we got in back.

"I didn't introduce my friend," he said, indicating the KGB man. "This is Filip Ivanov, who will be our companion and guide through the bureaucratic labyrinth. Unfortunately, he speaks little English."

"Enough," Ivanov said. "Understand more than speak." He was looking straight ahead through the windshield, expressionless. "—There is no need for you to speak in Russian for my convenience."

He had a soft accent, unmistakable. "—Are you from the Ukraine? Kiev?" It was the wrong thing to say.

"*Da.*" He turned slowly and nailed me with cold black eyes. "—An unusual talent for a foreigner. You have studied the regional accents of the Soviet Union?"

If I say I studied it in college, he'll ask the name of the professor, and by nightfall I'll be . . . "—Not formal study. Just a hobby." I demonstrated: "—This is Byelorussia . . . this is Moscow . . . this is your Kiev . . ."

"—And yet you yourself have a Leningrad accent. As if you had been born here."

My God, could they already know? "—My first Russian teacher was a Leningrader . . . high school . . . what was his name . . . ?" Saved by the horn. The other KGB man pulled up behind us in a small black, dusty Volga and bleated three times. Menenkov put the car in gear and pulled smoothly away.

It was a fairly long drive into the city, during which we occupied ourselves with conspicuously safe conversation. Menenkov had been to both Washington and Helsinki, and we discussed the relative merits of the two places. He wanted us to compare Miami with Washington, and Valerie unleashed her considerable powers of sarcasm. That was handy, because his responses gave me the measure of his grasp of colloquial American: complete.

He was quite a likable man. That could turn out to be a problem. After I finished my performance at the summit, heads would roll.

The Leningrad Hotel is about twenty years old, faded but modern. Decorated by Finns, it could pass middle-class muster anywhere in Europe or America. We were given a suite overlooking the Neva, at the spot where the old cruiser *Aurora*, whose guns signaled the beginning of the October Revolution, sits anchored. The suite had a sunken tub, Japanese style, but the tap water was rusty. Radio in the headboard of the bed, which I assumed was two-way. In spy novels and movies there's supposed to be one bug you can find right away, one that you have to really search for, and one that only the audience knows about. Concealed in the molar of the glamorous KGB woman you're taking to bed. Alas, not this time.

But we did assume that everything we said would be monitored, quite possibly by the Americans as well as the KGB. So if we had anything interesting to say, we communicated by note. (I'd brought along a couple of small tablets of cigarette papers for this purpose; they burn away completely.)

We were free until evening, so we bundled up and strolled along the Neva for a while. Still a few stubborn patches of ice. I ached to point out to her things I remembered from childhood—places I'd last seen as fallen rubble, now miraculously risen. But we had to be circumspect. That parabolic reflector we'd bought for the rebuilt machine could have picked up clear speech from half a mile away, and the KGB has probably surpassed Edmund Scientific in that area.

She started to tire after a couple of miles, because of the previous evening's excesses. I walked her back to the Leningrad and then returned to the subway station near the bridge. Restlessly manifesting a classic approach-retreat behavior pattern. I wanted to see my home, yet I was desperately afraid of what I would see.

The subway system was much extended from what I remembered as a boy. The map I'd picked up at the hotel was a sketchy abstraction. I chose a new station that had to be in the right part of town, and plunged on down to the train.

The subway was beautiful and scrupulously maintained, perhaps a hundred times cleaner than Boston's. A thousand times cleaner than New York's. Of course, a person who was insane enough to pull out a can of spray paint would be summarily tossed onto the tracks, and not by the police. The people are proud of their subway. If you so much as drop a gum wrapper, somebody will growl *"nikulturny"* and drag you back to pick it up.

I got off two stops past Nevsky Prospekt and was disappointed to see new buildings. But there were older ones, vaguely familiar, off the main street. My memory was not as sharp as I'd thought it would be. There was a cabstand outside of the subway stop; I got in the first car and gave him the address I remembered from a half century before. "—Is it still there, Comrade?" I asked.

He turned and gave me a half smile. He was about my age, grizzled but neat in a frayed way. "—You sound like a Leningrader."

"—Yes, of course." In Russian the phrase is ambiguous. I tried to give him a KGB stare, with no answering smile. "—So do you."

He shrugged and started the car. "—All I mean is . . . it's hardly three blocks away." He looked at me in the rearview mirror. "—Do I take you or give you directions for walking?"

"—Take me. It's been a very long time."

The building where I had lived was gone, replaced by a modern box of glass and steel. But Alex's, the one that Nazi bombs had blasted flat, was standing there again. Like a corpse made up to look alive, rouged in quiet repose. The building glowed in the slanting evening sun, and in a terrible rush of memory I realized it had been this time and this season when I'd heard the crash and run outside—and there in the roiling sparkle of dust and the threnody of the maimed and dying, there was Alex's father with his bloody burden. He was himself wounded, which I had forgotten for some decades; scalp torn and half of one ear ripped away. Now there was dry dust in the air again, the smell of pulverized concrete, and though it was from construction this time, I still saw ghosts and burst into tears.

After a minute the driver spoke softly. "—Comrade. Do you want to get out here?"

"—No. Take me back to the Metro." He had to go three times as far to return, because of one-way streets and signs forbidding left turns. When he pulled up to the taxi stand, I thrust a handful of rubles at him and tried to get out, but the door wouldn't open.

He came around and opened the door and helped me out. Then he put his hand on my neck and carefully pushed the rubles deep into my coat pocket. "—It was a very short drive. How are you living?"

In Russian that's a stock "hello" phrase, but it can be more. "—I'm living well," I managed to respond, and patted him on the shoulder before fleeing downstairs.

On the subway, the people politely did not stare at my tears. It was not the unusual sight it would have been in America. We Russians are an emotional people. Perhaps I should not say *we*.

When I got back to the Leningrad, I tiptoed by Valerie and tried to take a nap, but woke up after an hour drenched in sweat, an unspeakably bloody nightmare fading away.

Surprisingly, it was not about Alex or my old home. It was something about an arm. A bloody, disembodied arm.

CHAPTER THIRTY

Jacob

JEFFERSON AND I were making a career out of chasing false Foley leads. Most of them cleared up with a few phone calls, though we did take trips on government expense to Cincinnati, Akron, Lincoln, and fabulous Gary, Indiana. No leads would ever show up in New Orleans or San Francisco, or any-place else fun.

We were sitting in the Cambridge office, I picking my way through a Soviet journal of behavioral psy-chology, Jefferson poring over a lurid magazine called *Full Auto*, which was not about cars. It taught you how to use machine guns in various social situa-tions. The phone rang.

It was Langley: Harriet Leusner of the Foreign Re-sources Division. "Jacob," she said, "I have a man you're just dying to meet."

I sat up, electrified. "You've got Foley?"

"Not actually. Someone almost as good. Why don't you come down and talk to him?"

"Who is it?"

"Let me be mysterious. I want to see your reac-tion." She could be infuriating. "Call when you get manifested and we'll have a car waiting for you."

I hung up. "Let's hit the road, Jefferson. The wild goose calls." He unfolded from his nearly horizontal reading position and loped to the closet. He pulled out our two overnight bags, nowadays always packed and ready, and his heavy artillery and Kevlar vest. He always dressed informally around the office, just the .44 Magnum and whatever he had tucked away under his clothing. Probably enough to take out a platoon of Viet Cong. I didn't want to know.

We had it pretty well figured out by the time we got to Leusner's office, but seeing the bastard in the flesh was a shock nevertheless. Mikhail Shilkov, a.k.a. the Scalpel. We didn't offer to shake hands, just stared. He looked like Peter Lorre with Charles Manson's eyes. Jefferson said his name.

He was sitting in a straight-backed chair with two men flanking him; Leusner sitting behind her large, clean desk. "You may know Herb Stratton, from the FBI," she said. I nodded at him; we'd talked on the phone a few times. "And this is Andrew Coleman, also from the FBI. His function is similar to Sergeant Jefferson's." He was not quite as big as Jefferson, but equally well padded.

Stratton spoke up. "He walked right into Washington headquarters and surrendered. He wanted to make a deal."

"Come on." Jefferson put my thoughts into words. "We don't make deals with this kind of scum. Do we?"

Coleman smiled at that—it was their line of work this guy was debasing—but Stratton scowled. "For some things we'll deal with the devil himself. Shilkov said two magic words."

"Nicholas Foley," Shilkov said. "I can tell you where to find him."

"I'd rather let him go," I said to Leusner. "Harriet, this guy is—"

"We know what he is. There's a lot at stake."

I looked at Shilkov. "What kind of deal do you want? Plea bargaining for torture and mass murder? Mutilation?"

"I did not really do that," he said in a rasping voice. "Not under my own volition. Foley ordered me to do it. My own . . . comrades." He shook his head in a pretty good simulation of controlled grief. "Besides . . . can you think that I am that stupid? Killing four KGB agents, two of them in cold blood!"

"We don't think you're stupid," Jefferson said in his best Dangerous Black Person accent. "We think you're crazy as a *bed*bug." He continued in flowery Russian: "—Compared to your inhumanly cold-blooded evil, even a Rasputin would look like a simpleminded *stilyagi*. Don't insult us by playing the innocent."

"I don't speak Russian," Harriet said coldly.

"Just amplifying my sentiments," Jefferson said, still staring at Shilkov.

Shilkov stared back. "I will not talk with this black man in the room."

"Suits me." He reached inside his jacket, and I tensed. He took out a miniature tape recorder and set it on Harriet's desk. "—Speak clearly, comrade." He turned and stomped out, remembering to open the door.

"You can go, too," Harriet said to Coleman.

"He's very dangerous, ma'm," Coleman said.

"This *room* is dangerous. Don't worry." He left.

"He asked for you specifically," Stratton said. "He knew from someone that you were the person who'd been involved with Foley the longest."

"Your Roberta Bender is a double agent," Shilkov

said. "I give you that for free. I have much more to give you."

"Tell me something I don't already know. She's flown the coop. You must be out of touch with your own people."

"Yes. Since the day of the . . . unpleasantness."

There was an empty chair a couple of paces away. I dropped into it. "Unpleasantness. Sometimes this business makes me sick."

"He wants to trade," Stratton said. "He cited the Witness Protection Program."

"So he spills his guts and we give him a new identity," I said. "Relocate him in some small town somewhere."

"Exactly," Stratton said. Shilkov's English, his American English, probably wasn't good enough to catch the grace note in that one word—the inflection that implied "exactly *not*"—but it reassured me.

"Okay. Sounds like a fair trade. If he does know more about Foley than we do."

"I know a great deal more. I saw him at the factory in Cabin John. He doesn't look at all like his pictures. I can identify him for you. I may be the only person living who can."

"Back up," Stratton said. "Weren't you *here* to find him?"

"Yes. Find him and kill him."

"But you let him go," I said.

"This is where the story gets fantastic," he said.

"At first we didn't recognize him. He's lost fifteen kilograms, shaved off his beard, cut his hair. And we'd overheard him, by listening device, tell another agent that he was not Foley, but a private detective in Foley's hire.

"I had no reason to disbelieve him, and began interrogating him as if he were the detective. He . . .

turned the tables, though, and started giving *me* orders, and I had to obey."

He held up his left wrist, showing an ugly ridge of keloid tissue. "He made me do this, try to kill myself. After I'd . . . taken care of the others." He sat up squarely. "Your black man accused me of being evil. I have done some extreme things in service to my country. But nothing like Foley. Foley is a madman."

Maybe it takes one to know one. "All right," I said, "but what we're really interested in is exactly where Foley is, and how we can safely approach him. Can you tell us those two things?"

He swung those eyes on me. "I think I can tell you where he is. How to approach him safely . . . I would have an expert sniper shoot him dead from no closer than a hundred meters. And have another sniper covering the first."

"So where do we find him?" Stratton said.

"I will tell you once I am convinced that your Witness Protection Program will hide me from my own people. Not until."

Harriet picked up the phone and punched four numbers. "Eric, it's me. Have you cleared that FBI package?" Pause. "Okay, bring it on up." She looked at Shilkov. "This will give you a start. But you have to cooperate; you have to keep a low profile. You start tearing small animals apart and we don't know you. Or you'll wish we didn't know you."

"There is no need to be insulting—"

"I'm just trying to be *clear*. If you break any civil law, you're in very grave danger. And not from the KGB. We and the FBI have our own processes and resources to protect, and the last thing we need is publicity about them. Is that *clear*?"

"Don't worry. Even if I was not afraid of you, I would be afraid of my own people."

"You'd best be afraid of us as well." There was a knock at the door. "Eric? Come in."

A bespectacled apparition about seven feet tall and weighing half as much as me pushed open the door and slipped in. He had a manila envelope in one hand and a regular business envelope in the other. "Shilkov," he said softly.

"I am Shilkov."

"Not anymore." He walked across the floor with no sound. He handed Shilkov the manila envelope, and when he grasped it, the dry, crumpling noise was loud. "I don't want to repeat myself, so listen carefully. You are Harold Samuelson."

"Harold Samuelson."

"Your New England accent is much more pronounced than the residue of Slavic. So your documents say you came from Boston. You were born and raised there. We're dropping you in Indianapolis. You have two years of college and have most recently worked as a truck driver, chauffeur, and taxi driver. All in New England. You will seek employment as a taxi driver once you know your way around Indianapolis. Your Boston references in that regard are safe." He looked at me. "Mr. Bailey will cover them for you."

"That's all in here?"

"Yes. Papers and cards. All of the cards in that envelope are what we call flash . . . alias . . . documentation."

"Flash alias documentation."

"That means they're only good for identification. There are two MasterCards and a Visa in there, and two gasoline cards. Don't try to use them. If you charge anything on them, we will come kill you."

"All right."

"That was a joke. But don't use them. In this envelope," he handed over the small one, holding it by the corner, "there are two cards that are 'back-stopped,' as we say. The Visa card has a prepaid credit line of three thousand dollars. Once you have used that, you're on your own. The Gulf card is over-paid by two hundred dollars and registered to your Indianapolis address. It would be smart to use these to get more plastic in your own name."

"I know. Americans swim in a sea of credit."

"Yes. And you are an American. If you forget that, you may die." He stared at Shilkov, as still as a stalk-ing bird. "That is not a joke."

Shilkov stared back. "I'm a Yankee Doodle dandy," he chanted in a monotone. "Yankee Doodle do or die. A real live nephew of my Uncle Sam. Born on the Fourth of July."

"Very good." He looked at Leusner. "May I go?" She nodded and he slipped out, looking carefully neutral.

Leusner opened a drawer and took out two fat letter-sized envelopes. "This is your walking-around money for Indianapolis. Twenty thousand dollars in fifties and twenties, in each. You get one when we catch Foley. The other, you can earn today."

"I'm at your service."

From the same drawer, she produced a yellow pad and a mechanical pencil. Standing, she pushed them over toward him. "Names. All those names you claim to have. Name, function, location, cover. Addresses would be nice."

He picked up the pencil and clicked it a few times. "With forty names, that's only five hundred dollars per name. Surely I'm saving you—"

"We're saving your life. Any more complaints and I'll just send you downstairs to the torture chamber."

"Come now. You don't—"

"We built it just for you."

"Yes, of course." He picked up the pad. "Is there a room where I can be alone?"

She nodded and stood up. "Follow me." They walked out, and Stratton and I sat in silence for a few seconds.

"I don't like this at all," I said. "We shouldn't give that man anything but the electric chair."

"Not to worry," Stratton said. "Harriet will fill you in."

"What is it?"

He chuckled. "It's Harriet's game. It's sweet. She'll want to tell you herself."

Leusner came back in, looking satisfied. "So what is it?" I said.

"That guy Eric." She sat down and spun around in her chair. "We've known for *three years* that he was working for the KGB. Feeding him stuff that's neutral or false. Sometimes important stuff that's true, when we know it was compromised by someone else, or it's about to go public.

"The timing is great. He really has outlived his usefulness; we know from another double agent that the KGB has tumbled to the pattern. So the last thing he does will be a favor to both of his employers. Finger that bastard."

"So we'd better find out all we can before he goes to Indianapolis."

"That's right," she said, smiling broadly. "Cab drivers have accidents."

CHAPTER THIRTY-ONE

VALERIE

IT WOULD BE good to visit Leningrad when I didn't have so much to worry about. They had put together a sort of "wives' tour" with an unrelentingly cheerful Intourist woman and a kamikaze bus driver. So we learned all about the *Aurora* and the October Revolution and the Summer Palace and we saw the mammoth in the deep freeze and tried to absorb all the art in the Hermitage in three hours, paintings flickering by like the frames of a Saturday-morning cartoon.

It's hitting Nick hard. Not the tension of the upcoming confrontation. He lives for that kind of stress, though he'd never admit it. It's this country or this city, his childhood memories. Well, nine hundred days of absolute terror and deprivation. After almost ninety days of it myself, I had some inkling of how they feel. Everyone you meet over fifty seems to radiate memories, the permanent existential bruise of having survived the war. Everyone under thirty radiates impatience.

Sometimes it feels like the whole country is a monument to the Great Patriotic War, and the old men in charge use it as a guilt trip on the young. Waiting

in line at a cafeteria, I met a woman who was studying English at the university, who was bitterly sarcas-
tic, whispering, about the new war memorial being
constructed out in the suburbs. She and her boyfriend
had been trying to get an apartment for three years, so
that they could get married and not have to live with
parents. But no, there had to be another granite slab
of Socialist Realism, in the middle of dignified acres
that should be holding up apartment buildings.

It's like a person who survived having a cancer cut
out and keeps the damned thing in a jar, showing it
constantly to his children and neighbors. Don't
smoke. Eat lots of fiber. This could happen to you.

And yet you can't criticize it, not from the outside,
no more than you can tell a widow to stop grieving.
We went to the Piskarevsky Cemetery, on the out-
skirts of the city, where most of the people who died
in the Siege are buried. Symbolic gravestones and
marble plaques on the ground, not identifying indi-
viduals. No one knows how many lie there. More
than a million. Acres of rolling fields with carefully
spaced trees. A memorial building full of terrible
photographs: piles of bodies, buildings exploding,
fires and ice. A crying woman pulling a child's sled
with the child lying on top, rigid in death. When we
left, it was raining and the sky was almost black.

Back at the hotel, Nick was sitting at the window,
staring out over the Neva. He asked me where I'd
been, and I told him, and he burst into tears, silent
tears.

He tried to laugh it off, through the tears, saying
he'd had too much vodka with lunch, and the sadness
of the city was getting to him. Maybe that was for the
benefit of the microphones. Maybe it was for me. But

he should know that after twenty-five years a woman can tell when her man has had a drink.

Something is gnawing away at him, and we can't talk about it. Not just because of microphones.

CHAPTER THIRTY-TWO

NICK

I HAD TESTED the watch against President Fitzpatrick while we were "alone," carefully; asking him direct questions that would normally generate indirect answers, and it had worked. It also worked well with the translator, Menenkov, and his two KGB men. Today I would find out whether Vardanyan was hard of hearing.

We were taking over the swank Petrovksy Restaurant on the tenth floor of the hotel, all of the *apparatchiki* from both countries who had to make their importance known by bending elbows with the most powerful. Premier Dr. Vardanyan would be there, since he happened to be in the neighborhood, on his way back from meeting Fitzpatrick for their symbolic reunion in Germany. Fitzpatrick couldn't make it, of course, but Vice President Aldrich appeared as if by magic.

I was beginning to recognize in myself an unreasoning prejudice against people in rumpled dark suits with thin black ties and smirks. They were much in evidence. There was always one in the elevator. Always one in the men's room. Always in the bar, in the lobby, in the tearoom. Somebody hand me the Raid.

When the vice president and his entourage showed up, I was waiting in the lobby, as requested; I was to be his translator. It was surprisingly easy to get him alone; his Secret Service guard had to go upstairs to report to someone. (You could tell that Aldrich was miffed at that. I could have been a dangerous spy.)

It was easy to test the watch on Aldrich because he was a smoker. With smokers, I'd just say, "Give me a cigarette,"—not "please do you have . . ."—and when they held it out, I'd say, "No, take it back." If they did both without reaction, I could be pretty sure the watch was working; if they did react, I could cover myself by saying, "Sorry, I'm trying to quit. Not quite myself." Aldrich handed me a cigarette out of a tooled leather case and put it back without comment.

"Who's minding the store?" I said. "You here and the president in France."

"Spain. Actually, Fitz is still running things. Wonders of modern science. Briefing by satellite every morning, Cabinet meeting before dinner. All unclassified, of course; walls have ears. After lunch he usually gets in touch with me and Seales." Peter Seales was the press secretary.

That he called the president Fitz was revealing. That was his "political" nickname, I'd found out with the watch; his friends called him Gid.

Valerie was waiting for us at the head table, along with Menenkov and a few Special Assistants for This and That, American and Russian. I introduced her, my Linda, and Menenkov, and we joined everybody else in waiting for Vardanyan.

A formal Russian dinner is more fun than an American one, though to appreciate it fully requires more tolerance for alcohol than I have. A long trough set in the center of the table was filled with shaved ice, cooling three different kinds of vodka, two varieties of Soviet champagne, and, incongruously, many long-neck bottles of Pepsi-Cola, legacy of Armand Hammer. Most of the Russians were drinking Pepsi, and most of the Americans champagne.

Menenkov greeted me warmly and poured me a glass of champagne. "I'm afraid it's not Mumm's, Anson."

"I know." I took a small sip. Sort of like carbonated Thunderbird. "When do you expect Vardanyan?"

He spread his hands. "His plane came in three hours ago." I knew that, of course. "He may be resting."

"What if he rests till midnight?"

"—Hunger is the best sauce," he said in French. I couldn't remember whether I, as Anson Rafferty, spoke that language. I smiled noncommittally.

"In America, the guest of honor usually shows up late," Aldrich said. "Is it that way here?"

"Sometimes," Menenkov said softly, comically slewing his eyes from left to right. "Sometimes he doesn't show up . . . at all."

I laughed, and so did Aldrich, uncomfortably. "Your friend Ivanov is conspicuous by his absence." The Ukrainian KGB man.

"Only so much room at the table." He poured himself some more champagne. "I assure you he is here in spirit. So to speak."

I raised my glass to him. "—As some of my friends must be."

"What was that?" Aldrich asked.

"Old Russian toast," I said. "Absent friends."

A festive Russian meal would normally be many hours of eating and drinking. You start out with what would be considered appetizers in other countries' culinary traditions—bits of smoked fish, small boiled potatoes in sour cream, pickled vegetables, caviar rolled in small pancakes—and you follow each tidbit with a shot of ice-cold vodka. The vodka's less than seventy proof, but a lot of it goes down in the course of a couple of hours' nibbling. Then the main course comes out, perhaps a stroganoff or baked stuffed fish or fowl, along with wine. Then a sweet and brandy. Then more brandy and whatever vodka's left. Then you try to remember whose flat you're in and what your own name is, just in case.

Our banquet was going to be more Western style, but they did bring out token plates of traditional appetizers. Menenkov was demonstrating to me the correct way to roll up caviar in a pancake when everyone got to their feet. Coming through the door, Vardanyan told everyone to sit and strode toward our table, trailing a quartet of bodyguards.

He greeted Menenkov by his first name and shook hands with the vice president, speaking rapid-fire Russian. "The premier welcomes you," Menenkov translated, "and thanks you for having been able to grace us with your presence on such short notice." Vardanyan had taken three years of English in school, according to the CIA, but didn't speak it well. There had been periods in his life when it wouldn't have been *safe* to speak English well.

For a long second he studied me, focusing the considerable force of his personality. He was a small man, with features invariably described as "hawk-like": sharp beak nose, sloping forehead with a sharply defined ridge of bone under eyebrows that looked like stiff filaments of white wire, curling. He was almost completely bald, his skin was wrinkled and spotted with age and work, but his eyes were cool, clear gray. I translated Aldrich's polite response, and he nodded, looking abstracted for a moment. Then he turned his attention back to me.

"—They tell me you used to work for the CIA."

"—Yes. In Germany, back in 1962 and—"

"—Do you work for them now?"

"—No. Nor any other intelligence agency." Unless you count the KGB, technically.

"—And you are independently wealthy."

"—My wife is."

He smiled, almost wan. "—Then can you tell me why you took General Lambert's job?"

"—He was sick, he asked me. Also, I've never been to Russia." I turned on the watch. This had to be done delicately, with all these people listening who knew Vardanyan more or less well.

"What's the premier talking about?" Aldrich asked, breaking my concentration.

"Small talk, sir. He's asking about my . . . qualifications." Menenkov whispered a translation to Vardanyan.

"—Yes, qualifications," Vardanyan said, putting the tips of his fingers together. "—I find it remarkable that the president would choose an ex-CIA man, however skilled an interpreter he might be."

"—I never was a CIA man, actually. I was a private citizen working in Germany, and the State Department asked me to dig up some information. I only later found out that the CIA was involved." By pushing my wrist along the tablecloth a few inches, I could turn the gain all the way up. "—I assure you that you can trust me completely. I'm a good American but not political. My primary allegiance is to mankind in general. You must believe this if we are to work well together."

He rubbed one finger up and down his long nose,

staring. "—For some reason I do trust you. You are a most persuasive man." I turned the gain down. It might be suspicious if everybody at the long table went along with what anybody else said.

Vardanyan spilled some caviar on a pancake and rolled it up one-handed, John Wayne style. He smiled at Aldrich and said, "Now to the serious business of eating," with an accent as thick as the Neva outside.

CHAPTER THIRTY-THREE

JACOB

WE HAD TO go into Washington to find a store that carried Shilkov's vile French cigarettes. He was going to have a hell of a time getting them in Indianapolis. Maybe he'd live long enough to kick the habit.

We had him sequestered under discreet but heavily armed guard in a condo in Vienna, Virginia. The Agency owned the top three floors; the doorman and the elevator operator were GS-8 muscle.

In two days, we rounded up more than forty of the agents he'd named. I was dying to interrogate him about Foley, but Leusner asked us to hold off. She had to go to Berlin for a series of meetings, and wanted us to wait so that she could be in on it. I think she also wanted at least some of the leads not to pan out, to give us some leverage on him.

So for most of a week, Jefferson and I sat in the room next to his and read, watched television, played cards for matches. Each match was worth a million dollars, and Jefferson won not quite enough to pay off the national debt. We shouldn't have been wasting time, though. Shilkov did know where Foley was, or rather, he guessed right, and it was no place obvious. Except now, in retrospect.

Four days. What would the world be like now if we'd traced him down and stopped him?

Leusner went straight from the plane to Langley, and straight from Langley to the Vienna condo, and walked in unannounced on our game of million-dollar whist. Her face was puffy with jet lag. She was holding the envelope of "walking-around" money, the bribe.

She slapped the heavy envelope against her palm, twice, smiling wearily. "Shall we?" We tossed down the cards, and Jefferson put on his coat.

Ironically, Shilkov was watching *The Price is Right*, perhaps in the spirit of trying to understand his newly adopted country. He was engrossed and looked up, startled, when we came in through the connecting door. Leusner turned off the television and sat stiffly on the edge of an easy chair.

"Most of the leads you gave us have been successful." She took a slip of paper out of her breast pocket and glanced at it. "Except two here in Washington. Can you tell us anything more about James Edward Wentworth or Suzanne Lin?"

"You didn't find them?"

"No. Wentworth flew the coop; his apartment's clean. Lin went out to a movie and never came back."

He shrugged. "Washington's a small town. When you started picking people up, the word must have spread."

"I suppose. Have you found the look-alike?"

"None exact, of course. I narrowed it down to three." We'd given him some photo albums the FBI supplied. They weren't criminals, just people with various facial characteristics, photographed from the

front, and side. Shilkov had MALE CAUC BLOND
50–60, MALE CAUC WHITE 50–60, AND MALE CAUC
BALD 50–60. All three were in the blond volume;
Jefferson and I had seen them two days before.

She looked at the nondescript pictures and shrugged.
"Okay. So where is he?"

He leaned back on the couch and laced his fingers
together. "I thought that you would never ask. He is
in Russia. Leningrad, or headed there."

We all stiffened. "The summit," Leusner said.
That was the next day.

"You could have told us earlier," I said.

Shilkov smiled sweetly. "As I say, you never
asked. I think you made a point of not asking."

"How do you know he's going to the summit?"
Leusner said.

"The woman. Valerie Foley. She doesn't know she
told me anything."

"So you didn't force it out of her," Leusner said.

"Oh no, not in the sense of torture. In fact, I never
hurt her at all—though I did threaten to; that's part of
the technique."

"Go on."

"We gave her only water for a couple of days. I
. . . worked on her resistance with various psychologi-
cal devices. Finally we gave her water that contained
a hypnotic. When she fell asleep, I injected her with a
compound the KGB's Special Services technicians
made up, called Batch Seven. It lowers one's antago-
nism toward interrogation."

"Like Pentothal?" I asked.

"Somewhat. People don't babble so with it. It's
almost like normal conversation."

"Makes torture obsolete," Jefferson said. As usual,
Shilkov ignored him.

"But wait. She wasn't in contact with him until the

Cabin John thing, right? Your people in Boston had her."

"That's correct."

"Then she couldn't know where he was going. She couldn't know about Leningrad."

"Ah. This is where you have to trust my expertise. My knowledge of human nature. Especially when it comes to people lying, or telling the truth."

"Go on."

"I found that she knew nothing more about Foley's power than we did. As I told you a few days ago. But I went a little further, and told her what we suspected: that Foley had somehow discovered or invented a technique or substance or device that completely subverted a person's free will. That it would make him do exactly what Foley asked, even kill himself.

"She said she had suspected that for some time, from various questions we had asked. But it wasn't anything she had any knowledge of."

He took out a yellow cigarette and tapped it on his thumbnail, inspected the end, and lit it carefully with a wooden match. "And so I asked her about herself. What would *she* have him do with this power?" He watched the match burn almost to his fingers, then dropped it in the ashtray.

"Go to Leningrad?" Leusner said. "Disrupt the summit?"

"Not exactly. I'm only inferring that. What she said specifically was that he could get into government, wind up next to the president, talk him into making peace. She thought about it some more and said that he wouldn't have to limit it to the president of the United States. He speaks so many languages so well, and so forth. She had a high opinion of him.

"She even mentioned Russian specifically, and Vardanyan. I didn't think much of it at the time, since

there was obviously no way Foley could get within
ten kilometers of the premier without permission.
Later, after Cabin John, I thought about the summit."

"That's fantastic," I said.

He smiled, a baby's plump lips. "Consider it. How
many people go along with the president? A planeload? Two planeloads?"

"It's just possible," Leusner said. "According to
her profile, she was very passionate, even fanatical,
about peace, and I think he may be, too."

"That's all over his MIT dossier," I said. "He jokes
with his students about marrying a hippie, about neither of them ever recovering from the sixties."

"Worth checking. Jefferson, you get in touch with
the Secret Service and get all you can about everybody going to the summit with Fitzpatrick. Better ID
all the press, too; I suppose they'll have a separate
plane. Use my name freely, but don't tell anybody
what you need the information for." Jefferson nodded
and headed for the phone in our room.

"Bailey, you go through State and try to get us
diplomatic clearance into Leningrad. We get into the
visa red tape and the Soviets will hold us up till Labor
Day, on principle, if they smell the Agency."

She stood up and dropped the envelope into Shilkov's lap. "If we do find Foley, you're free to go.
Eric Langer, the quiet, tall fellow from our Technical
Services section, will bring your tickets and instructions." Shilkov started to say something, but she
turned away abruptly. "I'm bushed. Is there an unoc-
cupied bed around here?"

"Sure; follow me." I led her into the bedroom. Jefferson's bed was made up with military precision;
you could bounce a quarter off it. I was obscurely
gratified that she chose my rumpled one.

CHAPTER THIRTY-FOUR

NICK

IT GAVE ME an odd feeling to be in a room with six KGB men and six of their American counterparts, CIA and Secret Service. It was the room where the "confidential" part of the summit talks would be held. All twelve were presumably electronic entomologists. Menenkov and I had been invited to watch the proceedings, as nontechnical witnesses. He seemed amused but alert.

The Russians had proposed a fine old nineteenth-century drawing room in the private part of the Hermitage, which the Americans instantly vetoed. Full of nooks and crannies and doubtless already wired for sound with fifth-generation Japanese smart bugs. The Americans suggested an unornamented Finnish-modern meeting room at the Leningrad, overlooking the Neva, but the Russians said "no windows." They said the Americans could bounce a laser off the glass from orbit; pick up the speech vibrations. The CIA men laughed and said they wished they could. (I would have assumed that particular trick to be physically impossible, if they hadn't laughed.)

The two teams finally reached uneasy agreement, settling on a modest interior meeting room in the

Leningrad. All the rooms on its floor and the floors above and below were emptied, mutually inspected, and sealed off, which meant that half of our protocol team was sent grumbling to the Metropole downtown.

They wouldn't have to stay there long, though. This was April 29. The back streets of Leningrad were filling up with provincial marching bands practicing, athletic teams going through routines, and elaborate floats decorated in themes of *mir,* which in Russian means both "peace" and "world."

If things go well with Vardanyan and Fitzpatrick tomorrow, they'll have something to *mir* about.

I took a nap after the debugging session, knowing that Fitzpatrick would be coming in around seven. The dream came back again. I think.

Nothing like this has ever happened to me. I appear to be having the same dream, or a dream about the same things, every time I get into REM sleep—and then I strongly suppress the dream upon awakening, or before. It must be a memory of Leningrad, but a bloody arm? I would remember it if it were significant. There are a hundred memories from that time I would suppress if I could. Plenty of disembodied arms and legs, sometimes heads, sometimes worse. I learned what the female genitalia look like from the immodesties of two frozen, shattered bodies, entwined. That is a memory that comes back unwonted.

The cliché truism that people who gravitate toward the study of psychology do so because they are profoundly hurt in their own minds. . . . I know from observing my colleagues that there is more than a grain of truth in that, and of course they know it from observing me. What if they found out I was a murderer, a spy, and a megalomaniac out to change the world? Some would shrug and say, "What did I tell you?"

I was with the party that met the president at the airport, but we only exchanged a cursory greeting as I introduced Menenkov. He then drove to the hotel with a limo full of advisers, having no need for a translator. I went back with Menenkov.

We drove for a while in companionable silence. "It is frustrating," Menenkov said. "When I began training for this job—as a child, really, just after the war —many people were saying that the United States was going to emerge a huge and powerful empire. Having suffered no damage in the war, having all of its industrial capability intact."

"That's about what happened."

"Well . . . it's not 'empire' the way I mean. Some of our people do talk about the American empire, meaning your country plus all the client states embraced by NATO, SEATO, ANZNAT, the OAS—"

"Not the most loyal clients."

"I know. That's what I mean. The American hegemony that we were going to face, it's not really there. It's as if you took aim at a target, and as it drew near, it broke up into many targets of various sizes. Still one largest piece, but the others can't be ignored." He laughed. "I should not indulge in metaphor in a foreign language. I don't mean shooting at you."

"I think I understand. But should you be saying this to an ex-CIA agent?"

"You're right, it hardly seems fair. Since I have myself never had anything to do with the KGB." We both laughed. "What I mean is that, in a curious way, it would be easier for us to negotiate if it had come about that way. America a monolithic power, with no complicating alliances."

"Some country has a proverb saying you should choose your enemy well, because you're fated to become him. Is that Russian?"

"Probably. I could never keep them all straight." He tapped on the steering wheel with a ring. "That can be taken two ways. Do you want to become like us?"

"I don't know Russia well enough to say," I said, and the truth startled me.

"Perhaps we can compromise and each wind up with the best of both worlds. No McDonald's."

"Okay, and no so-called champagne." We laughed together. I turned on the watch at its highest setting.

"Can I see Vardanyan tonight, with you along, and nobody else?"

"That shouldn't be any problem."

"Can we set it up so that it's in a 'safe' room, where we won't be overheard?"

"I can't speak for the CIA. No KGB will be listening."

"You are a KGB officer yourself."

"Of course."

"What rank?"

"Major general. I am the highest-ranking KGB officer in Leningrad, currently, I believe."

"Wonderful. You will arrange this meeting tonight under some reasonable pretext. Then come get me."

"All right."

"You will follow these orders but forget that I gave them to you. You will not recall any of this conversation since I said, 'Can I see Vardanyan tonight?' "

"All right."

I turned off the watch. "Looks like rain."

He peered up through the top of the windshield. "We should just make it."

CHAPTER THIRTY-FIVE

JACOB

THERE WAS NO way the State Department could officially get us to Russia the day before May Day, short of stuffing us into a diplomatic pouch. But the CIA does have resources.

A Lion's Club tour group was delayed by engine trouble in Los Angeles long enough for me to fly to Seattle and intercept them, bearing passport and visa that had been routinely processed "just in case." I was a Lion from Marlow, Oklahoma. I hoped nobody would question me about that. Do they still have cowboys and Indians down there? Are they rich with oil money? I'd have to make up answers.

By way of cover, they gave me a handful of Southwest Equity Insurance Company business cards and a fake-leather Traveling Presentation Kit. If anybody got too curious, I would start selling him a policy.

There was no trouble from my fellow passengers, though. The airline had provided free drinks during the delay in Los Angeles, and there had been a party. When the plane picked up our small contingent at Sea-Tac airport at midnight, only the crew were conscious. When the Lions woke up the next day, flying over the Arctic, they were subdued. There was an in-flight movie where the main character was a car. During it I memorized large parts of *Fodor's Russia*, especially the street map of Leningrad, since I would have to break away from the tour group and rendez-vous with Harriet. (Actually, we should have wound up in the same hotel.)

We spent a couple of hours in Helsinki, waiting in lines, and then there was a short flight to Leningrad, and the fun began.

Six lines through Passports; I chose the shortest one, which turned out to be the longest. After an hour I finally got to the glass booth. A nineteen-year-old KGB private said, "Pazz board," and I gave it to him. For a good two minutes he didn't look at it, just stared at me, unsmiling, directly at my face. I assumed he did that with everyone, and returned his stare with a pleasant smile.

"—You speak Russian, don't you?" he said in a sudden loud, staccato voice, accusing. I tried not to change expression.

"I'm sorry. I don't speak Russian."

"—You aren't fooling anybody." I guessed this was also part of his routine. He went through my passport page by page, though it was newly issued; blank except for the small stamp on the fourth page, from Helsinki. Suddenly he glared up at me. "Ah!"

He pulled a hand mike from the wall. "—Please, Captain, there is an irregularity, Kiosk Four." He hung the mike back up and redoubled the intensity of his stare.

After a minute the captain showed up. They exchanged whispers while he stared at me from his loftier rank. He also scrutinized my passport and then put it in his shirt pocket.

He stepped out of the booth. "Follow me," he said

with an accent good enough for Hollywood. "Bring your luggage."

We walked away from the luggage-inspection tables and down a corridor that smelled of mildew and vinegar. "In here." He opened a door. "Wait."

A table and two wooden chairs under a bare hanging light bulb. A toilet and wash basin in a dingy alcove. No windows. The door closed behind me, and he locked it with a key. I leaned against the table and waited uneasily. What could they do to a CIA agent entering Russia illegally? I knew what they could do. They could make me disappear, and the Agency wouldn't peep. Wind up working on a hydro-electric project in Khatanga until I froze solid, which would be sometime in early June. Or they might try to trade me for a couple of real spies.

Interesting thought: I could finger Shilkov for them. All I want is my freedom and a Hero of the Soviet Union medal.

After some rattling and muttering the door creaked open and the KGB captain returned, followed by a skinny man in a dark suit. "Sit down." I did, and the captain sat across from me. He leafed through the passport and stared at the first two pages.

"Who is the mayor of Oklahoma City?"

"How should I—"

"Your passport was issued there, was it not? It is the capital of your state."

"But I've only—"

"You were born there." To the man in the suit he said "—He lives outside the biggest city in his state, the city where he was born, but he cannot name the mayor."

"My parents moved away from Oklahoma when I was two," I said rapidly. "I hadn't set foot in the state until I moved back there last year."

"—He says that . . ."

"—I understood. Ask him why he joined the flight in Seattle. Los Angeles is closer to Oklahoma." The captain translated the question.

"I have friends there. It didn't cost much extra. What is all this about, anyhow? Do you take one person every hour and give him the third—"

"Not at all," said the civilian in thick English. "Show him."

He opened the passport to the picture on the second page. "Look at this." He ran his fingernail under one edge, and it came loose. "I have seen many thousands of American passports. All had pictures very firmly glued down."

Oh, shit. Superspy. "I—I wouldn't know anything about that. I thought they came that way; I've never had a passport before."

"Yes, of course. But you must see that if this truly was not your passport, it could be the case that . . ." he paused to retrieve the subordinate clause—"You have taken the original picture off and glued yours on, but . . . without enough glue, or the wrong glue. You see why we are suspicious?"

"Look, though." I grabbed the passport and ran my finger along the embossed stamp that covered both the photograph and part of the page. "How could I fake this? It says . . . 'Department of State, United States of America'—how could I fake that?"

"I'm sure there are ways." He looked up at the "civilian."

"—It's probably nothing. You'd better have the forensic people look at the passport, though. And search his luggage very thoroughly, and his person." That sounded like hours. Not to mention Siberia.

"I'm afraid we will have to detain you for a little while," the captain said, putting my passport back into his pocket. "I will send somebody with a cup of coffee and a roll." He stood up.

"Hold it." I stood up, too. "I'm with a tour group. Are you going to hold all of them up too?"

He picked up my suitcase. "Arrangements will be made."

After about an hour, my coffee and roll appeared. They looked an awful lot like lukewarm tea and a piece of black bread. Better than nothing. I worried for another hour about being searched, which I was sure would include a colonoscopy with a dimestore flashlight, but when it happened, I wasn't even made to undress. An unsmiling lieutenant patted me down in a desultory way and left without a word.

I'd first gotten in line at eleven; at four, an Intourist lady showed up with my luggage and passport and no apologies. She led me to the moneychangers, where I got a hundred dollars' worth of good, soft Russian currency, and then I was given my very own tour bus, evidently the one that had taken the other Lions into town earlier.

She said our hotel had been taken over by American government people here for the summit, but we were going to have a much nicer hotel in the center of the city, the Astoria. Full of history and Old World charm. That was nice, but I was supposed to meet Harriet at the ninth-floor tearoom of the Leningrad Hotel, at four, six, or eight. Maybe I should argue, hey, *I'm* an American government person . . . no.

It was a long drive through cold, gray rain. No Russian road signs, no billboards to break the birch-and-pine-forest monotony. Decades after conjugating my first Slavic verb, I finally get to Russia, and it looks just like upstate Michigan.

CHAPTER THIRTY-SIX

NICK

THE DREAM WAS especially bad last night. I woke up three times, always with the bloody arm fading from memory. In the last two, there was somebody with the arm, brandishing a knife. I had hoped to get plenty of sleep for today's challenge. Not to be. But I had a long soak, and Valerie gave me a good rubdown. We talked about where we might be next week. If we don't wind up in custody by this afternoon.

Through Menenkov and Vardanyan, I had made certain arrangements with the Soviet press, and their American and European counterparts knew that something was up. I spent most of the morning strolling from room to room with my watch, making sure the fourth estate of the Free World would not be scooped by the likes of *Pravda* and *Izvestia*. By noon, everybody knew that something big was coming down, but nobody who was constrained by the truth could claim any details or reliable attributions. I assumed that by the time of the meeting, two o'clock, people's imaginations would have taken care of that.

The Americans got together at noon in a small banquet room for roast beef sandwiches and potato salad, courtesy of the White House cooks, which seemed strangely exotic after all the caviar and pickled vegetables. Valerie and I were not seated with Fitzpatrick, who was going over last-minute details with his aides. In a few hours they were going to wonder why he'd withheld his blockbuster. But that was consistent with his personality. He has a liking for grand, dramatic gestures.

There was only one small detail to take care of before the meeting. After lunch there was a punch bowl and a semblance of relaxed mingling. I kept my eye on the Secret Service men, waiting for one to isolate himself. Finally Jerry Kepperman, the second in command, drifted over to stare out the window. I sidled up next to him and turned on the watch.

"Do you have a second, Jerry?"

"Sure, Dr. Rafferty. What's up?"

"I want you to find me a small pistol. Something I can stick in my belt or pocket without being obvious."

"No problem. Little revolver in my ankle holster." He started to reach for it.

"No, not now. In two minutes, I want you to go to the men's room next door. I'll meet you there."

"Okay."

"You won't remember any of this. Nothing I said to you. Just follow directions."

"Okay."

I went straight to the men's room and waited. It was dirty, but not as noisome as most of the Soviet public bathrooms I'd been in, a concession to the hotel's foreign guests. There was nobody there, but I had to assume there were listeners.

Kepperman came in, and I motioned him over to the urinal. I flushed it and whispered in his ear, "Go into the first stall and take off the pistol and ankle holster. Leave them on the floor." He nodded and did it, muted rip of Velcro. When he came back, I flushed again: "You will remember having loaned the pistol to another agent. You'll get it back tonight."

"Okay."

"Go back to the luncheon now." He did. I went to the stall. I hoped that if there were hidden cameras or people peeping, they didn't have the insides of the individual toilets covered. If they were being *that* thorough, I was done for anyhow.

Snub-nosed Colt .38 Special. Six shots; six more in a rubber loader taped onto the side of the holster. Not much protection against the Secret Service and KGB collections of Ingrams and Kalishnikovs, but I didn't really plan to shoot it out with anybody. I just wanted an edge.

I strapped the pistol onto my ankle and came out of the stall. Still alone. For the hundredth time I looked, and the envelopes were still in my inside coat pocket, untouched. For the hundredth time my fingers found the throwaway plastic glove in the other pocket.

There would be no fingerprints. One envelope and its contents were authentic White House stationery, typed upon by a White House secretary. The other, which had been harder to arrange, was heavyweight Russian bond, transcribed from my handwriting by a secretary in the Soviet embassy in Washington.

Perhaps we had been careful enough. If we hadn't, well, at least I wasn't unarmed.

Menenkov and I got there a few minutes before our charges. The room was bare, scrubbed too clean. There was something in the air that made my eyes hurt. "—Are you nervous?" he asked.

"*Da.* You've done things like this before?"

"Not this scale. I've worked with Dr. Vardanyan in

French and Polish, and with some other people in English." He shook his head slowly and continued in Russian. "—But nothing really like this. The importance of it makes me a little sick. What if I make a mistake?" He made a helpless fluttering gesture with his hands and switched back to English. "I can't help thinking: This is my children's future. Even though the meeting is largely symbolic."

He stood up and walked three paces to the wall. "My own life is . . . has been . . . more than adequate; I have no complaints. But I have a boy who's just started university, and a girl . . . who is still a girl. It's their future. I worry."

"No need to worry, not about language. We can backstop each other. You know the phrase?"

"I get the sense of it, yes. If one of us makes a mistake, the other can point it out, and there's no harm."

"That's right."

"True, and thank you. But I woke up this morning thinking I would much rather read about this in the newspaper than be part of it. Don't you feel that way?"

I didn't have to lie. The door opened, and Vardanyan and Fitzpatrick came in, along with Kepperman and a Russian guard. We stood for the leaders. The guards waited until they both sat down and then backed out to rejoin the other guards outside.

Each of the four places at the table had a yellow tablet, pencil, pen, and an agenda typed in both languages. Fitzpatrick picked his up and scanned it. "Most of this is *pro forma*. It's only the last three we really have anything to argue about, right?" I translated.

"—That's right," Vardanyan said. "—I still have some reservations about Item Six, 'Trade restrictions on potentially sensitive industrial products.' My advisers are uncomfortable with the wording of that. But it's something for specialists to work out; I think we agree on the sense of it." He smiled thinly. "—If not the necessity." Menenkov translated.

For about an hour the two men sparred politely, mostly over trade relations and human rights. Long enough. I took a deep breath.

I turned on the watch at its highest setting. Put on the plastic glove and took out the two envelopes. Vardanyan was starting to speak. "—Excuse me," I broke in. "—I'm in charge now."

The two Russians nodded. "What's up?" Fitzpatrick said.

"Just a minute." I handed Vardanyan his envelope. "—Please read this very carefully."

"What's the glove for?"

"Fingerprints." I handed Fitzpatrick his envelope. "Read this carefully. You're about to deliver it as a speech to a couple of billion people."

Fitzpatrick didn't take the envelope. He just looked at me. "What the blazing hell are you talking about?"

I'd never actually had my blood run cold before. It's an accurate expression.

Fitzpatrick started to rise; half-turned toward the door. I dragged the .38 out and cocked it. "Don't. If you call out, I'll kill you."

He sat down slowly and looked at Vardanyan and Menenkov. Vardanyan was reading, and Menenkov was watching the scene with detached interest. "So what's the matter with them? It's as if . . . oh, no." He covered his eyes with a large hand. "You're the guy the CIA's after. Folly, Foley. How the hell could you get into this room?"

"That's not important."

"You must have had control over me back in Washington. Why doesn't it work here? *Hear*ing, that's it!"

God, would he have to die for deducing that? "What do you mean?"

"Ear infection, then the damned pressurization in Air Force One—I've got tinnitus real bad; loud, buzzing sounds and ringing. It must interfere with whatever you do."

I motioned with the gun. "Read the speech."

He picked it up. "I'll read it, out of curiosity. I won't deliver it for you." He stared at me. "I don't think you'll kill me. But if you do, you do. I accepted that as a condition of employment years ago."

He read through it carefully and set it down. "Vardanyan has the same?"

"Yes. I wrote Vardanyan's and my . . . a person familiar with your style wrote yours. He will deliver his speech even if you don't do yours. That would set up an interesting situation."

"I would almost do it just to see what happens. But no. Vardanyan will deliver his, and . . . it will be explained away. He cracked under strain. He's an old man."

"We'll see." Keeping the gun trained on him, I went to the door and opened it partway. "Kepperman? Would you come in here for a moment?"

The big man came in, looking cautious. I told him to close the door behind him.

"You're carrying that Ingram, right?"

"I am."

"And guarding Mrs. Fitzpatrick."

"That's right."

"The president is supposed to give a speech within an hour. If he doesn't, I want you to kill Mrs. Fitzpatrick and then use the Ingram to kill as many other Americans as you can see."

"All right."

"Do the same if anything unpleasant happens to me—if I am taken into custody or killed, I mean."

"All right."

"You will forget that I gave you these orders. They will remain in force until I instruct you otherwise." He agreed. "Leave."

That had been a gamble. Fitzpatrick had watched in shocked silence. If he'd started giving conflicting orders, I don't know what would have happened.

When the door clicked shut, I suddenly felt faint. I had just arranged for the murder of a dozen or so innocent people. If Fitzpatrick stuck to his principles or the CIA or Secret Service found me out or if I had a heart attack, which right now didn't seem too unlikely. I floated back to the table, not really feeling the floor under me.

"You're a monster," Fitzpatrick said.

"I think I know what I am." Vardanyan was looking at me with a bleak expression, looking just like my stepfather, and as I sat down slowly, the dream rushed in, the first time it had invaded my conscious mind:

I was eight years old and starving, gone beyond hunger to dying, bloated weakness, so cold that my breath glazed into ice on the metal bedframe, and there was a candle in the kitchen, a small, wet noise, and I crawled along the cold floor to see, and watched for several minutes while my foster father carved a half-frozen bloody human arm into chunks of meat for the pot, a bloody soldier's sleeve on the floor with a red star on the shoulder, and we had "lamb stew" for the next two days, and it was good past belief, and nobody questioned where the lamb had come from.

Fitzpatrick was talking. "What was that again?" I said.

"You have to call him back in and cancel that order. Admit your plan has backfired. So far you haven't done any harm. I can guarantee . . . the best of treatment for you."

"Oh, I've done harm."

"Even if I *do* give your speech, what makes you think I can implement it?"

"Two billion witnesses. And the fact that Vardanyan is saying the same thing."

"But *I* know! Sooner or later the whole world will know where the speeches came from."

I had an answer to that. I was trying to shake off the nightmare image, the memory of the taste. "I can . . . I can answer that." The unspeakable guilt of cannibalism, repressed; was that behind everything?

"Sooner or later your hearing will recover. When that happens, I can change your recall of these events. Meanwhile, I'll stay very close to you."

"How close do you think you can stay? For how long?"

Inspiration: "Dr. Vardanyan is going to invite you to his *dacha* to the south of here, for a few days' rest. You don't want to fly for a while, after all, because of your ear infection. Of course most of your entourage will stay with you. Including me and Mr. Kepperman."

"You have it all figured out, don't you."

"Except for a few details." Like what to do with the memory of the taste.

CHAPTER THIRTY-SEVEN

JACOB

FODOR'S HAD WARNED me about how beautiful Leningrad was going to be. I'll have to go back someday when I have the peace and clarity of mind to appreciate it. They say it reminds people of Amsterdam, so Amsterdam must be full of potholes and noisy construction—and yes, stately symmetry and impressive public parks and monuments. Nice bridges. But I spent a lot of time looking at my watch.

The bus driver parked in front of the Astoria and left the engine running, putting a much-handled cardboard sign on the dashboard. Knowing I spoke no Russian, he herded me into the hotel lobby and waited in line with me until he could get a clerk's attention. He told the clerk that I was with the earlier group of American Tigers or whatever, and then stomped out the door to retrieve his bus.

In carefully weird English, the clerk explained what I was to do. I was sharing Room 364 with so-and-so, but they were all out on a tour. I could leave my bag in the room and then I would be free to do whatever I wished, so long as I left my passport with him and my key with the "floor lady." Better than I'd expected. In five minutes I was back on the street. There were four cabs waiting in front of the hotel; I got in the first and asked for the Hotel Leningrad, speaking no Russian.

I probably got a special non-Russian rate, since it was a short ride for twenty bucks, but I didn't think it would be smart to argue with him.

The lobby was full of American and Russian security types. An American turned toward me; I took a chance and gestured imperiously, beckoning him to a quiet corner. I wished I'd had some of Jefferson's physical presence and *chutzpah*. I did my best, though: "I don't have time to discuss this much. I'm a CIA man and I'm supposed to make a contact here, an American woman. You want to help me?"

"You have any ID?"

"Come on."

"Well, look. Things have been really complicated since they cut the meeting short. I've gotta—"

"Cut it short?"

"Yeah, Vardanyan left. Some press thing coming up—look, you can take the elevator there up to anything past the seventh floor and nobody'll bother you. Below that, above here, you need credentials. I've gotta get my men together." He turned and went back to his group.

That was all right. When the elevator came, it had the buttons for two through six removed, and a couple of armed guards, just in case you'd brought your own button. I pushed nine and tried to whistle. My mouth was too dry.

I asked the guards which way the tearoom was. The American shrugged, and the Russian stood impassive but pointed to the left when the door opened.

It was more than an hour after our designated time, but Harriet Leusner was there, sitting alone at a table for two, seemingly engrossed in a paperback book. She saw me and waved.

"Jake, I thought you'd *never* come! Here's your book." She handed me a paperback that was slightly open at the last, blank page. There was writing on it: *I don't know what the hell is going on here, and I don't think anybody really does. Vardanyan's headed for the Summer Palace for a TV announcement, before six. Fitzpatrick's going to do the same thing, here. You go catch V's speech, and I'll wait here.*

No sign of anyone who looks like F. Keep your eyes open.

I scanned it fast. "Uh, fine. Look, I gotta run. Catch you here this evening?"

"Yes, in a couple of hours. Go on."

I got back in the same cab, since he had gone to the back of the short line in front of the hotel. He took me back across the river and dropped me at the large crowd that was forming where Vardanyan was to speak. I pretended naïveté and told the driver I was running out of rubles—how much would that be in dollars? A thoroughly illegal transaction, but it saved me fifteen bucks.

I dove into the crowd and started working my way toward the front, looking for a blond, portly middle-aged American.

CHAPTER THIRTY-EIGHT

NICK

I USHERED VARDANYAN and Menenkov out and told the press liaison woman that Fitzpatrick would be resting for a half hour before he delivered his statement, and that he might or might not talk to the press after that. I used the watch on White House Chief of Staff Froelich, to make sure no one on his own team would bother Fitzpatrick.

Then I went back in and sat with him, giving Vardanyan time to get to his press site across the river.

"I suppose you do mean well," he said. "But I don't think you're aware of the potential for disaster in this . . . speech."

"Why don't you outline it for me?"

"I can't give you an education in geopolitical realities in the space of thirty minutes."

"You don't have to. I've already spent thirty years thinking about it. Peace and war and what could be done. And spare me the old-soldier bit—I was in the war, too, and hurt a great deal worse than you were."

"You can't be old enough."

I grabbed a pinch of the firm skin under my chin and wiggled it. "Plastic surgery. They can work wonders."

"That's why. . ."

"Yeah. I haven't been myself lately." He argued with me for about fifteen minutes, appealing variously to common sense and patriotism and arithmetic. Then he fell silent and read the speech through a few times. When he delivered it, he actually made some improvements.

This is what he said:

I am aware of having some few shortcomings, and one that doesn't normally bother me much is a lack of oratory ability. I think the shorter the speech, the better, and don't have much patience for politicians who go on and on just because they have the floor.

But this is one occasion where I could wish that I had the gift of eloquence. Nothing I will ever do or say as president of the United States of America can be as important as what I am going to say to you now. Forgive me for saying it plainly.

Everybody knows that the large and fairly equal nuclear stockpiles held by the United States and the Soviet Union have been for half a century rather a "mixed curse," paradoxically threatening the survival of the entire world while apparently preventing a catastrophic world war from starting. The key phrases our politicians have traditionally used to describe this curious situation are the frightening ones "the balance of terror" and "mutually assured destruction."

It's also well known that these stockpiles are, and have been ever since the sixties, much larger than they would need to be if their function were simply military. Grotesquely large.

Both the Soviet Union and the United States possess more than a hundred times the megatonnage required to obliterate the other's civilization totally. It's hard to imagine: more than a hundred times.

Most of the presidents and premiers from Truman and Krushchev to Dr. Vardanyan and myself have agreed that these weapons must never be used, and pledged that we would not initiate the use of them. Pessimists in their turn, from the 1950s to the present day, have pointed out that this may be fine for the next week or year, or ten years or a thousand, but sooner or later there will be a man or woman in charge who will suffer a lapse of judgment, a lapse of sanity, and actually use the weapons. That will be the end of civilization, or at least all that we hold civilized. Perhaps, some of our scientists warn, it would be the end of all life on this planet.

The problem with idealistic solutions to this situation, where we simply wave a magic wand and all the bombs go away, is twofold: One, as I said, the bombs with their threat of apocalypse have brought comparative peace to the second half of this century. Two, the United States and the Soviet Union are not the only ones with bombs.

Dr. Vardanyan and I were both soldiers in the last world war—what we hope will forever remain the last world war. No one who lived through that catastrophe could take lightly the obligation of preventing his children and their children from having to relive it. And if it takes the fear of nuclear Armageddon to keep buried in history the specter of whole continents turned into battlefields, of whole generations of men decimated and decimated again, then that fear does serve a noble purpose. If Dr. Vardanyan and I *could* wave some magic wand and rid the world forever of nuclear weapons . . . well, I won't say we wouldn't do it. But we certainly wouldn't do it in ignorance of the possible dire consequences.

What we have agreed upon is a mutual bilateral reduction in the size of our strategic nuclear forces. A drastic reduction, conducted simultaneously, under the supervision of observers from countries aligned with neither the United States nor the Soviet Union.

The third largest nuclear power in the world is Great Britain, with two hundred and ninety-eight warheads capable of delivering ninety-nine megatons of destruction. That is the level to which Dr. Vardanyan and I have agreed to reduce our forces. Nearly a thousandfold. By May Day of next year, both the United States and the Soviet Union will control only two hundred and ninety-eight warheads apiece, yielding a total of no more than ninety-nine megatons.

The distribution of these weapons as to size and type will be worked out according to the defense requirements of each country, but the total number and total yield will be the same. Both countries will undergo continual inspection by neutral observers. In agreeing to this, Dr. Vardanyan has of course departed drastically from the policies of all his predecessors, and the world owes him a vote of heartfelt thanks.

The disarmament process need not be frozen at this level. If Great Britain wishes to reduce its nuclear forces below their present capabilities, and if they will do so under the same conditions of supervision and inspection that Dr. Vardanyan and I have agreed to, then the United States and the Soviet Union will also reduce, to maintain parity. If the British consequently fall below the strength of the fourth nuclear power, which is currently France, with two hundred and two warheads yielding ninety-two megatons, then France will be responsible for setting the benchmark. Then China, then India, and so on down the line.

It isn't a perfect solution; there is no perfect solution. A lot of voices will be raised, and some heads will doubtless roll, in the process of turning this, our mutual pledge, into diplomatic and legal language satisfactory to all concerned. But the principle is clear, and we will not back away from it.

At this moment Dr. Vardanyan is delivering a speech to the Supreme Soviet in Moscow, via a public television link from the Summer Palace here in Leningrad, outlining our agreement. Journalists are present from all over the world, and the message is being broadcast live on every Soviet television channel.

We want to give the world some breathing space. The principle we've set down here will certainly be elaborated and refined by leaders of our countries, of all countries, in the future. What we have tried to do is to ensure that there will *be* a future.

They'd set a rostrum up right in front of the meeting-room door. I stayed in the room, with the door open a crack, so I missed seeing the president's face and nuances of gesture. But I could see the expressions on the audience's faces, which was amusing, and Valerie's, which was gratifying.

A small room full of hardened pols and newspeople, with a scattering of Secret Service, KGB, and CIA folks. When he said the words *mutual bilateral reduction,* a lot of jaws dropped open. When he elaborated on it, some people looked like they were going to faint. At the end of his speech, about half the audience burst into wild applause. The other half clapped politely and belatedly and looked at each other in wild surmise.

CHAPTER THIRTY-NINE

JACOB

WITHOUT CEREMONY, VARDANYAN walked up onto a hastily erected podium, into a glare of television lights, to the exact spot where Lenin had stood the day the Soviet Union was created. That was what the man beside me told his companion, at least. I wondered whether Lenin had also spoken from behind bulletproof glass.

Vardanyan's speech may not have been more important than Lenin's, but it certainly was more surprising to the audience. Not so surprising to me. So Foley had gotten to him.

I wondered whether Fitzpatrick had said the same thing, as advertised. There was an American television team on the other side of the square; I meandered over there and eavesdropped. It was true, according to what their opposite numbers at the Leningrad had told them. Foley had flummoxed the two most powerful men in the world into renouncing the main basis of their power.

What the Politburo and the Congress would have to say about their agreement was yet to be heard. Maybe Vardanyan was headed for a long rest cure. Maybe Fitzpatrick, too.

There were no taxis, but then I guessed there was no need to hurry, either. I walked back down the river toward the bridge to the Leningrad, a mile or so. I was passed by groups of people running in both directions, a lot of happy talking and shouting and passing around of bottles. A lot of *mir* in the air. Even though it was still light, several barrages of fireworks went off over the river, setups, I suppose, that were supposed to wait until tomorrow.

I checked my watch, subtracting seven hours for Eastern Standard Time. The *Today* show and *Good Morning America* would be on in twenty minutes. Their staffs were probably quite busy.

I was tired and wired. I put my last No-Doz between two back teeth and crunched down. The overwhelming gall taste always reminded me of undergraduate days.

Nobody paid any attention to me as I walked up to the Leningrad Hotel entrance. Security people had formed up in a double line so that the luminaries could make it to their limousines, running the gauntlet of photographers. I overheard something about Fitzpatrick staying on in Russia for a few days. Probably a good idea. Probably a number of his compatriots will suggest that he take up residence permanently.

One advantage to being thin is that you can slip through crowds. It only took me a minute to make my way to the edge of the police line. Various people walked through the television lights, looking important. Then came Secretary Froelich, whom I recognized, and then the president, looking at the sidewalk with a sad smile. Behind him was a stranger. The stranger passed within two yards of me, looked straight into my face, and suddenly flinched and turned pale.

It was Foley, by God. It didn't look like him, but who else could it be?

I smiled and gave him a half salute, then watched the back of his head as he followed Fitzpatrick to the limo. He looked back once, and I was still smiling. Let him fidget.

I wasn't going to blow the whistle on him. Twice he spared me when he could have greatly simplified his life by killing me, at no danger to himself. Besides, it might work.

His cockeyed scheme might work.

CHAPTER FORTY

NICK Epilogue

IT WAS VALERIE'S idea. Where was the best hiding place for someone who could be history's richest and most powerful man, independent of any government? A haven of poverty and insignificance, of course, in the swollen heart of the bureaucracy itself: the Peace Corps.

For ten years, she and I toiled in the drought-scourged villages and farms of Rwanda, helping scrape irrigation systems out of the hard crust of the land, teaching English and numbers and our own version of The American Way. She was in her natural element, helping people. For me it was a long decade. As penance, though, I suppose it worked. The bad dream went away, and so did the killing. Though I don't think I would ever have tried to kill anyone without the watch, and it was in a safe-deposit box on the other side of the world.

Curiously, at the very end time of Valerie's fertility, she became pregnant. (When she stopped menstruating, we thought it was menopause. It was Nick, junior.) She delivered him in an American hospital, because of the possibility of complications, but we returned to Rwanda and raised Nickie in relative poverty. Being poor didn't impress him, of course, given his surroundings and companions; and we have tried to raise him in such a way that when he eventually finds out he has millions, that won't impress him, either.

I came back from Rwanda old and leathery but fit, weighing about what I did in Basic Training. We found a suburban community with good schools and bought a carefully modest house. I took one certificate of deposit out of the safe-deposit box and spread it around several local banks. I took the watch out, put a fresh battery in it, and hilariously tested it on Valerie. Then I returned it to the box, along with the millions in CD's and securities that had grown from the cash left over from our second round of plastic surgery in Zacatecas.

It looks as if this twenty-first century may turn out better than the previous one. The four largest nuclear powers playing a reverse Mexican standoff, just as Valerie had predicted. Usually it's France who ditches a warhead, just to make the others scramble. It's always a small warhead. But every year there are not quite as many bombs around as there were before.

Of course there are still wars, and rumors of war, and we may yet live to see nations consumed in nuclear fire. At least it won't be the whole planet burning. Not so long as they follow the rules of the game.

But treaties are only promises, and promises are only as good as the people who make them. The warhead factories can be started up as quickly as they were shut down.

This boy of mine is twelve years old. He speaks Russian and French as well as his native English and Swahili, and he keeps the ability secret. His childhood tempered with poverty, he owes allegiance to no god or country or culture; he doesn't even think of himself as white.

Most people get a watch when they retire. He'll get his when I think he's ready to start work.